G R JORDAN

The Hunt for 'Red' Anna

A Kirsten Stewart Thriller

"We laugh at honour and are shocked
to find traitors in our midst"

CS Lewis

Contents

Acknowledgement

To Ken, Jessica, Jean, Colin, Susan and Rosemary for your work in bringing this novel to completion, your time and effort is deeply appreciated.

Novels by G R Jordan

The Highlands and Islands Detective series (Crime)

1. Water's Edge
2. The Bothy
3. The Horror Weekend
4. The Small Ferry
5. Dead at Third Man
6. The Pirate Club
7. A Personal Agenda
8. A Just Punishment
9. The Numerous Deaths of Santa Claus
10. Our Gated Community
11. The Satchel
12. Culhwch Alpha
13. Fair Market Value
14. The Coach Bomber
15. The Culling at Singing Sands
16. Where Justice Fails
17. The Cortado Club
18. Cleared to Die
19. Man Overboard!

Kirsten Stewart Thrillers (Thriller)

1. A Shot at Democracy
2. The Hunted Child
3. The Express Wishes of Mr MacIver
4. The Nationalist Express
5. The Hunt for 'Red Anna'
6. The Execution of Celebrity

The Contessa Munroe Mysteries (Cozy Mystery)

1. Corpse Reviver
2. Frostbite
3. Cobra's Fang

The Patrick Smythe Series (Crime)

1. The Disappearance of Russell Hadleigh
2. The Graves of Calgary Bay
3. The Fairy Pools Gathering

Austerley & Kirkgordon Series (Fantasy)

1. Crescendo!
2. The Darkness at Dillingham
3. Dagon's Revenge
4. Ship of Doom

Chapter 1

Kirsten Stewart strolled down the middle of the East Gate Centre plotting a track straight to the store at the far end. It contained a myriad of clothing, foodstuffs, gifts, a little bit of everything. It had been one of those stores back in the day that was a leader of fashion, but its glory days were waning. She didn't dress there, genuinely seeking out more modern fashions, but if you needed staples such as underwear, there was no one better.

Her mood was good. She had spent a little bit of time with her London Man, as she liked to call him, and the quiet cabin they had cosied up together in had more than sufficed, being warm, with a well-stocked kitchen and a large roaring fire. She thought they were growing closer, having done all the things that younger people did when they fell in love. However, all the time there was that wariness, knowing that they didn't want to get too close in case the profession they were in took them away.

Kirsten's profession was operating as a spy, keeping an eye on Scotland, particularly the North, watching for any internal threats. With Anna Hunt, her dedicated and serious boss above her, and a small team she had assembled underneath, she'd already foiled several plots that if they had worked out would have been national news. At this time, though, there was little on the go, and she was taking the afternoon off, picking up the essentials before treating herself to a spa on the edge of town.

Kirsten entered the clothing department of the store and walked over to the ladies' underwear section before stopping in front of a rack, examining what she would have deemed to be sensible underwear. She thought back to the time away with her London Man and moved along three racks to underwear she thought were still supportive and neat. Also, they gave the air of a woman who could tease. She found herself laughing at her thought. Regardless, Kirsten picked up a number of items, checking the tags for size. As she did so, she caught a pair of eyes glancing her way.

Walking past was a man in a sharp suit and as soon as she looked at him, he stopped, turned, and picked up a number of underpants. She continued to stare and she saw him turn red and shrink before he said, 'For the wife's birthday gift.' Kirsten nodded and slid around the end of her rack but kept her eyes on the man. She drifted past him pretending to wander over to a rack with stockings. As she went past, she glanced down at the items the man was holding. His wife must have been one of those women who could simply shrink and expand on demand, for the bras he was holding ranged from a G cup back to a B. The hairs on the back of Kirsten's neck began to lift but she continued along to the stockings, sorting through them with no intention of ever buying any and then picked up the underwear she actually wanted.

She nonchalantly walked around the section, staring at the man, more and more convinced that he wasn't here for shopping. Time and again, he picked up items that were too varied in size and dimension to be for the same woman.

Kirsten stole over to a full-length dress mirror, stood in front of it and took her hair in both hands, pulling it tight behind her, before applying a hair tie. She could do this with her eyes closed but they were open searching the mirror for other people in the store. She saw the man glance across and Kirsten picked up a brunette woman, fairly young, and casually walking over to the section. Kirsten turned on her heel and strode over to the jeans' section, halfway across the store.

Once there, she saw the brunette woman approach, lurking at the far side of the jeans while the man who seemed so inept in buying underwear was now on the edge of this section of the store. Kirsten picked up several jeans and strolled to the changing rooms where she took a disc from a woman that had the number three on it, making her way to the far end, to enter a cubicle with a door.

Once Kirsten entered, she cast a quick glance back up the line of the changing room and saw the brunette woman enter, also holding jeans. Inside the cubicle, Kirsten dropped her trousers, knowing the woman might be walking past looking down to see if Kirsten was standing before the mirror. She heard someone close but Kirsten continued to stare at the mirror in front of her.

Pulling on a pair of jeans she had brought in, then moving this way and that, she pretended to examine her hips, looking to see if the item was fitting. As she bent down, giving the impression that she was seeing if she could crouch in the jeans, she looked in the mirror to under the door and saw the woman's feet. When they moved away, Kirsten stood up again, reached inside her leather jacket, and sent a text message that provided the name of the store and gave a call to arrive quickly. It was to her teammate Dominic.

If it had only been the woman, Kirsten wouldn't have called for Dom. She might have sent him a courtesy text to say she was being followed but she was confident in her ability to take on a single person. She spent the next ten minutes changing jeans over and over, seeing when one pair didn't fit, crouching down and watched feet moving backwards and forwards outside her cubicle several times. After the ten minutes she stepped out and waved to the attendant in the dressing room. She was standing with no trousers on, and the attendant came rushing down.

'Could you change these? I think these are slim fit. Could you get the wider ones so I could try them? If you could, I just don't want to go out there, obviously because I've got nothing on below.'

Kirsten gave a blushing smile, and the woman nodded politely, taking the items, and marching off into the store. Kirsten stood at the entrance to a cubicle pretending to watch for her return and saw the man at the far end peering in, neat with his short-cut hair and a chiselled chin. The suit he was wearing was loose presumably to cover any firearm he had underneath. Kirsten pretended to ignore him.

When the door of the cubicle beside her opened she saw the brunette lady step out. She was dressed in the clothes she had on before. When she saw Kirsten standing there, there was a brief moment of panic before she turned and looked away, shouting to the man at the far end.

'Size down from these, please, love.'

The man nodded and made his way back into the store. It was another two minutes before the member of staff returned, handing Kirsten her jeans, and Kirsten stopped her, engaging in conversation about the style and the cut. She was waiting for the man to come back. When he did so, she watched him bring a pair of jeans to the brunette woman, handing them over. Kirsten almost laughed. They were never a size down. If the woman stood up in those, they'd fall off her.

Kirsten politely thanked the member of staff, stepped back inside the cubicle, and pulled her own trousers on. She pulled her jacket over, stood looking in the mirror, waiting, until she felt her phone buzz. She picked it up and saw the message from Dom that he was inside the centre. Kirsten texted him back, requesting he make his way to the changing rooms on the west wall and gave a brief description of the man waiting.

Standing in front of the mirror, Kirsten ran her fingers through her hair. In case anyone looked in, she wanted to appear as someone vain. She pulled out a lipstick from inside one of her pockets. Not that she ever wore it, but sometimes, it was good cover. Standing there, her eyes watching the mirror behind her as she saw the brunette woman's hair passing along the top of the door, there was another text with a simple word. Apprehended.

Kirsten turned, pulled open her door, surprising the brunette woman outside. She didn't wait, but simply grabbed her, pulling the woman inside and shutting the door again. Kirsten spun her arm around the woman's throat before driving her to the ground. She pushed her close up into the corner, so the woman couldn't push away with her feet. With the woman's feet tucked up under her legs, Kirsten held her throat tight, feeling the woman's breathing slow until she passed out.

Kirsten searched her quickly, removing a gun and placing it inside her jacket. When several minutes later, the woman started to come to, Kirsten held the gun at her back, advising her that she was going to walk out of the shop with Kirsten, and if she didn't, Kirsten would act in a sharp and brutal way.

With her free hand, Kirsten texted Dom and he advised that Carrie Anne was outside with their van. Kirsten walked the woman from the changing rooms, thanking the attendant once again, and strode down the escalator and outside to the street where a workman's van was sitting, waiting, the rear of it having no windows.

The door slid back, and Kirsten pushed the woman inside before getting in herself. They were greeted by Dom holding a gun, and Kirsten saw the man who had been following her at the rear of the van, tied up with a gag over his mouth. Kirsten took some of the tape from inside of the van, tied up her own captive before putting some across her mouth. She sat down before opening the shopping bag she had carried with her.

'What's in there?' said Dom.

'None of your business,' said Kirsten. 'Essentials. Essentials I need to pop back in and pay for someday soon.'

'All right,' said Dom, and he looked away as Kirsten delved inside the bag.

'What put you on to him?' asked Dom.

'That man there,' said Kirsten, pointing at the bound man in the corner, 'has no idea about woman's sizes.'

'How do you mean?'

'G cup, D cup, B cup, all for the same woman. I bet you wouldn't make that mistake, Dom,' said Kirsten.

'I don't get the chance,' and Dom gave a grin. Kirsten could see the brunette woman looking at the man now, her eyes full of thunder.

'Yes, the jeans you sent him for, love,' said Kirsten, 'they'd have fallen off you. Apparently, you need to be a bit tighter on your cover.'

The van carried along for a good hour before coming to a halt, and the side door was opened. Carrie Anne, one of Kirsten's employees, gave her boss a smile. The blonde-headed woman was dressed snappily in a blouse and jacket, but she wore jeans and hiking boots beneath. It was unlike her. When Kirsten got out, she realised what safe house they were at. Stuck in the woods outside of Inverness, it was one of Kirsten's favourites, remote, and with a stunning view across the mountainside.

Dom brought their detainees out of the van, took them inside, and tied them to a couple of chairs. Carrie Anne put the kettle on, handed Kirsten a coffee and then Dom, while they stared at the people before them. Kirsten stepped forward, ripped off the tape from the man's mouth and bent down close to him.

'Okay, sunshine,' she said. 'Why were you looking at me? What have I done recently?'

The man said nothing and looked away.

'You're not in a good place,' said Kirsten. 'You realise that? I might let Dom here loose on you. See if he can free up that tongue.'

Again, the man looked away. Kirsten saw Carrie Anne step forward and rip the tape off the woman's mouth.

'How about you, princess?' asked Carrie Anne. 'You talk? She'll let Dom work on you as well. Won't be me. Or it might be worse. She might work on both of you herself.'

The woman stared off, not looking at Carrie Anne and Kirsten had a feeling about them. When you were trained, they told you to do that. Look away. Not to stare. Not to give anything up. Don't bait the person interrogating you. Don't play to them.

Kirsten reached inside the man's jacket, but only found a simple ID, a driving license which gave no indication of whom he worked for. When Carrie Anne searched the woman, again, only a driving license, nothing else.

'It says Alice here,' said Kirsten, looking at the woman. 'I take it that's a load of baloney as much as Dave over there. I think I know who you two work for. What I want to know is why you're following me.'

Kirsten turned away, made her way outside the house where she dialled a number for Anna Hunt. Her boss was rarely up in Inverness, basing herself out of Edinburgh, but Anna understood all operations that were going on in Scotland and often, much more. She was a good person to talk to because Kirsten had a feeling that these people were from the Service, or at least if not from her Service, from one of the friendly ones.

As she stood waiting for the call to connect through, Kirsten looked around at the mountains, seeing the grey sky hanging over them. When she'd been away with her London Man, the sky had been bright and crisp, and although the nights were cold, they had even managed the occasional walk. It had been a long time since she'd enjoyed nature in that way. You couldn't when you were stuck in a safe house, too many other things running through your head. After five minutes of calling, the number wouldn't connect to Anna Hunt. Kirsten began to get worried. There was a call from the door.

'What's the deal, boss?' asked Carrie Anne. 'What's up?'

'Anna Hunt's saying nothing,' said Kirsten, a frown on her face. 'It's not like Anna. It would route through to somebody else if she was unavailable.'

Together they made their way back inside. Kirsten sat on a table looking at her two captives until her phone rang. She picked it up and heard a voice on the other end. It gave a code. The male operator was very precise in giving it. He requested a code back and Kirsten did as asked.

'Miss Stewart,' said the man. 'You are requested to join Control at London. If you make your way to Inverness Airport, the charter is there already. If you could kindly arrange to bring our people with you, all will be explained at the far end.'

'Yes, of course,' said Kirsten and the call closed.

'What's up?' asked Dom. 'That's not a face I'm used to seeing.'

'Untie them,' said Kirsten. 'They're ours, or at least on our side.' Carrie Anne looked over suspiciously. 'It's true. Code from London checks out. We're off to Inverness, then down to London. You two can come with me. I want to know why we're being watched by our own side,' said Kirsten. 'I bet these two won't have a clue.'

Chapter 2

The flight down to London was conducted in near silence. The captured pair of agents said nothing, and barely looked at Kirsten or her colleagues on the flight. Kirsten placed a call through to Justin Chivers, the other member of her team in Inverness, whom she told to remain at base. Justin was not a field operative in the main and preferred to stay behind his computer, operating technical gadgets, or delving into records. Yet he was also someone who'd spent a lot of time with Anna Hunt, and Kirsten reckoned that bringing him to London could cause issues at that end.

On arrival at Gatwick, Kirsten saw her London Man, Craig, waiting for her. He was dressed in a sharp suit and on his face was a grimace. When she approached him, it was clear that he wanted to keep things professional; after all, that's what they'd said when they'd been together. In their private time, they could be intimate, they could be like real people, but when they met, working for the service, they wouldn't let any of it show.

'Miss Stewart, I am to take you to meet with Control; they need to have a discussion with you. They've asked that you don't bring anyone else.'

'They don't want Dom and Carrie Anne there?'

'It may be that they've never met Control and they want to keep it that way.'

When he said *Control*, Kirsten knew that Craig didn't mean a specific person. It could be one of a number of people, whoever's task was overseeing the current commission, whatever that may be. When she'd come previously to London, she'd met a man called Godfrey. Very old school, aristocratic, but Anna had been impressed by him and Kirsten wondered if Godfrey was now caught up in this. *What could they have against Anna?*

'Of course,' said Kirsten. 'Just give me a moment to talk to the team. I'll be with you.' Not giving her man a second glance, she strolled back to her team advising them of the situation.

'Oh, and you two,' said Kirsten, pointing to the agents they'd captured, 'why don't you show my guys where you get a decent cup of coffee here.' There were no smiles and besides, Kirsten knew they'd be heading off for a debrief, having to explain why they failed so badly in their task.

'Make sure you tell them about sizing a woman,' said Kirsten. 'Need to put that into the Basic Training package.'

'Do you think they're ours?' asked Dom.

'No, they wouldn't risk it, especially if they think Anna's involved in something,' said Kirsten. 'They'll be from one of the other agencies. Bit embarrassing though, getting caught out because you don't know your bra sizes or how jeans fit a woman.'

Dom laughed, 'You say that like it comes so easily,' then he reached over, tapping Carrie Anne on the shoulder. 'Come on, we'll head over to the terminal and wait for Kirsten in there. I take it you could be awhile, boss.'

Kirsten shrugged. 'I have no idea, but I want to know what's up with Anna. I've rung her and I can't get her.'

'Well, go find out,' said Dom. 'We'll be here.'

Kirsten watched the pair of colleagues march off together, both in good form. They didn't seem to have the feeling that Kirsten had, that something serious was up. She never had anyone spy on her before, at least, not from her own people.

Of course, that wasn't strictly true. When she protected the child in Stornoway, people had come from her own side. People that had gone bad, but Anna had stood up against that. While at times she could struggle to warm to the woman, Kirsten had every faith in her. It was troubling her now that she couldn't even get hold of Anna.

She returned to her London Man and he escorted her to a saloon car, parked high in one of the terminal car parks. Kirsten asked if she should sit in the front, so as not to make it look like some sort of diplomatic mission, and the man nodded. As they pulled out from the car park, Kirsten went to speak but the man held his hand up and pointed to a small circle on the trim in front of them. Kirsten nodded and said it was rather grotty weather they were having. The man nodded but slipped his hand across, placing it on Kirsten's thigh. She placed her hand on top of his, squeezing tightly, and they smiled at each other briefly, before taking up quite stoic positions again. *Even in the cars, they're listening to you*, she thought. *But they mustn't be tailing us. They must have enough trust in him for that.*

She stared over at Craig a few times, taking in the shape of his thick-set neck and the trim body that she had enjoyed only a week or so ago. He was barely in his thirties and London Man, as she affectionately called him, had only seemed too happy to be with her. They'd started it up as some sort of a way to have a break, no strings attached, both realising that they worked in a profession where you trusted so few people that you needed a release, somewhere where you could just be normal. But when they'd gone away, Kirsten found something else. She'd more than warmed to him. Craig was his name, his real name. He knew hers, for he'd been sent to collect her on several occasions, and she didn't have a secret cover within the agency, whereas Craig seemed to be known as *The Driver* amongst those he would pick up and take to places.

Craig drove the car away from Gatwick until they came to a wooded area. Kirsten saw a bald-headed woman, standing, waiting, at the far side of a car park. The car park was empty and there was light rain in the air as Kirsten stepped out. She pulled her leather jacket around her, for she felt cold and wondered if it was the weather, or just the look of the woman in front of her. Kirsten was small, not much over five feet, but the woman was smaller, yet she didn't have Kirsten's physique. Somewhat squat, more dumpy-looking than Kirsten, who at least had the trim body of a fighter, for all that she lacked in height.

'Miss Stewart,' said the woman, 'walk this way with me.'

'And you are?' asked Kirsten.

'Control,' said the woman. 'I'm running an op, looking into a mole in the service. It appears that mole is your boss, Anna Hunt.'

Kirsten stopped walking and turned to the woman. 'Anna, are you sure? She ratted out the last mole.'

'She did, but that doesn't prove anything. He was working independently of her, had his own agenda working for a common thug in Inverness. Anna, however, is on a much more serious scale.'

'More serious scale? In what way?' asked Kirsten.

'We believe she's a traitor. I've been tracking numerous agents' deaths over the last ten years, and Anna keeps coming up. And it involves Russia, their secret service, contacts made.'

'I didn't know Anna did any of that. I thought she worked up in Scotland.'

'She's been posted in Scotland for the last three years, but Anna works in a lot of ways. She has a number of connections in Russia which we thought were good, but it appears she might be a double agent, passing information back the other way.'

'And you have proof of this?' asked Kirsten.

'Proof is a difficult thing to come by. What we have is a large number of circumstances that cannot be explained, with Anna involved in every single one of them. She's the common thread. We've lost too many good people not to act.'

'In what way?' asked Kirsten.

'You have a new assignment, Miss Stewart. This one is above all else, and you'll not do anything else until you have completed this one. Am I understood?'

'Perfectly,' said Kirsten. 'What do I need to do?'

'There are no files for this job. You will report only to me. Is that understood?'

Kirsten was not happy with this, but she nodded. 'It's understood,' said Kirsten.

'You are assigned to eliminate Anna Hunt.'

Kirsten put a firm hand on the woman's shoulder, turning her towards her. 'Excuse me? I am to do what?'

'I thought the words were quite simple. You are to eliminate Anna Hunt.'

'Kill her?'

'Exactly.'

'You expect me to kill my boss?'

'She's no longer your boss. Have you tried to contact her recently?'

'Yes, but I couldn't get through.'

'Of course not, we've eliminated her phone network, those running through the department networks anyway. She'll have her own. There's no doubt you do. But you're not to contact her, you are to eliminate her. Do I make myself clear?'

'Why don't you bring her in? If she's done all of this, why is she not being brought in to be interrogated to find out where these double-crosses are happening?'

'She's too dangerous,' said the woman. 'And besides, it's not your decision. It has been decided that she is to be eliminated.'

'Do you have the file for the case?'

'No,' said Control. 'There is no file. We don't know who else she's working with within the Service. We've been watching you and your team.'

'Rather badly,' said Kirsten.

'That may be so, but we believe that you are clean. We still have eyes on our other teams in Scotland but as you are clean and you're able to get close to her, we are assigning you to eliminate her. You know her, you know her movements, you know her methods.'

'Do you have any idea where she is at the moment?' asked Kirsten.

'None. Again, that is your problem. Get this done, and get it done quickly, and then we'll move on.'

Kirsten was shaking her head. She couldn't believe what she was hearing. More than that, she'd never been used as an assassin. Yes, she had the skills to get close to people. She could take enemies out, she knew how to fire a weapon, she knew how to kill in numerous ways following her training, but these were generally done in self-defence. She wasn't one of the assassins within the network.

'Why don't you bring in the professionals for this?'

'Because Anna would see them coming a mile away,' said Control. 'She's a very dangerous woman. More dangerous than we suspected at first.'

'So, you have evidence? Maybe I could get that. It might lead me to where she is.'

'You have nothing but this instruction,' said Control. 'Do you understand that? You're to tell no one except your team, and you are to assess them.'

Kirsten thought about Justin Chivers, how closely he'd worked with Anna. Something didn't smell right about this. There's no way they would let Justin be involved, at least Kirsten wouldn't. Not when there's closeness because he'd been loyal to Anna before, ridiculously loyal. Maybe Control didn't know his secret, one that Anna did.

Within the Service, Justin was seen as something of a pervert, a man who liked the women, would ogle them, but he was tolerated because of his other skills. But Kirsten knew his real secret, about the man he lived with.

'Are you having problems processing this?' asked Control. 'You have your instructions. Kindly return to the car and get on with them, Miss Stewart.'

'Now you have to appreciate this is a bit of a shock, but I'll get it done,' said Kirsten. 'Don't worry about that.'

'Good', said Control. 'And you report to me, me alone.'

'And how do I contact you?' asked Kirsten.

'Call the main board at London. Ask for Stadia; it'll come to me.'

'Okay,' said Kirsten. 'You want me to go dark from this point.'

'Indeed. Don't call me until you have something.'

Kirsten nodded and turned away, trudging slowly back to the car. When she got there, she saw Craig looking at her with a concerned face. She gave him a nod, letting him know it was serious before sitting down in the car. He drove off, making their way back to Gatwick. As they did so, Kirsten reached over with her hand placing it on Craig's thigh. He dropped a hand off the steering wheel, taking her hand in his, squeezing it tight. *Anna Hunt*, thought Kirsten, *I have to kill Anna Hunt.* She knew her orders but felt they were going against every fibre in her body.

Chapter 3

Kirsten spent the return flight to Inverness in silence, refusing to talk to Dom and Carrie Anne about what she'd been briefed on, instead advising they would meet with Justin and discuss it as a team. It was difficult holding the information within and part of her just wanted the trip so she could absorb the information. Of all the people she knew in the Secret Service, and out of fairness, she didn't know that many, Anna seemed the least likely to betray it. She'd come through for Kirsten when it really did seem like someone was betraying the service and the woman was no-nonsense, but then again, that was how double agents worked, wasn't it? They gained your trust. They went above and beyond in the things that didn't matter to them, but not to their agenda.

As Kirsten poured over these ideas, she found her head spinning round and round, but her gut instinct kept saying Anna was clean. She thought of her old boss Macleod, back in the police force. He always had a gut instinct. He always made sure the evidence tallied up, always made sure that his instinct was simply a path to follow, not a conclusion.

As the plane touched down in Inverness, Kirsten could see Dom constantly looking over at her. Carrie Anne was slightly distant. Whether the team were just giving her space because it was obvious something complex was on her mind or whether they were unsure of their boss, Kirsten didn't know. By the time they reached the comfort of their own offices, it was eleven o'clock at night. The downstairs cover, the shop that they walked through every day, had been closed for a couple of hours. When the three of them reached the small conference room upstairs, it was only Justin Chivers and them in the building.

Justin was usually in a jovial mood, but instead, Kirsten could see he looked strained. He went to say something as Kirsten arrived. She merely put up her hand and pointed over to the coffee machine.

'Filled as ever, but what's this about?'

'What's what about, Justin?' asked Kirsten.

'Well, we're having a meeting at eleven o'clock at night. Dom said you didn't tell him what it was about, coming up.'

'We've had briefings before at eleven o'clock at night, important ones,' said Kirsten.

'Yes, but what's this one about?' Justin was insistent.

'What have you heard?' asked Kirsten.

'I don't want to say in case it prejudices you with what you're about to tell me.'

'If I tell you first, vice versa. So, what have you heard?' Kirsten stood staring at the man who first of all looked away and then back. 'They're after Anna,' he said. 'I've been told they're after Anna.'

'Who did you hear it from?'

'Friends inside the service. Not from Anna, before you think anything else,' said Justin.

'After Anna?' said Carrie Anne. 'What's this about?'

'What's she done?' asked Dom.

'Sit down. Bit by bit we'll do this. We're not having the rush of questions because I need to think straight. I need to get my head around this, too. I spent most of the flight trying to do it, but in truth, I'm still struggling with it. So, get the coffees over, sit down at the table, and I'll tell you what I know.'

With everyone sitting down at their respective positions around the table, Kirsten was able to tell of her meeting that day with Control. She went through detail by detail and also elaborated on what had happened earlier on in the day for Justin's benefit.

'What did Control look like?' asked Justin.

'Bald-head, woman who was smaller than me, older, middle-aged.'

'The two recruits that she brought in to try and observe you,' said Justin, 'what did they look like?'

Dom painted a picture of them both while Kirsten sat in silence. When he had finished, she looked over at Justin. The man seemed to be sweating.

'What's up?' asked Kirsten.

'I don't know her name, but the bald-headed lady, she's very high up. She works across different departments, possibly may have been brought in from outside. The other two don't ring a bell with anybody on our side. Did she say what Anna was doing other than giving away information that could have led to the deaths of different agents?'

'There was nothing specific,' said Kirsten. 'I felt like I got this little titbit so I was able to justify to myself why we should take her out.'

'Have you?' questioned Dom. 'Have you been able to justify to yourself? Because at the moment, I'm not.'

'You're not meant to justify it,' said Justin. 'It's a direct order, it's an instruction to kill her. We don't always work with the information. Everything gets compartmentalised. You know what you need to know. It's the strength of the service. It's also its greatest weakness.'

'What do you mean?' asked Kirsten.

'I've been in it long enough,' said Justin, 'to know when people get played. Never like this. They never play you to go and kill someone, but sometimes they've used one side of the service to do the dirty work of the other, and of course, you just get instructions.'

'Doesn't the higher up realise?' asked Carrie Anne. 'Surely they would intervene.'

'When Anna gave you instructions,' said Justin, looking at Kirsten, 'did you check about those instructions from up above?'

'No, of course not,' said Kirsten. 'I don't know who she gets her orders from. They could come from different places, different times. She's my boss.'

'Indeed,' said Justin, 'and here we have somebody completely unknown to us giving you instruction. What makes you think she's kosher?'

'Because we were being spied upon. We were being looked at, being vetted.'

'That vetting was brought to an abrupt halt because we simply captured her agents. Damn, sloppy work,' said Justin.

'I think I see where you're going,' said Dom. 'Logically, we have no evidence that Anna has done anything wrong. We simply have a kill order, but a kill order that's come from someone we don't know. The only thing that says it's legit is the fact that they were spying on us. If it's secret, they have to do it without informing a lot of people. This job that we do makes us the perfect target.'

'If we're being played,' asked Kirsten, 'what happens then? They would kill Anna and then they would come for us, wouldn't they, Justin?'

Justin looked over at Dom.

'I've got a bit more operational experience than Justin and yes, that's how I would play it. I would get those close to do the dirty work and then kill them off. Cover it up as either all being dirty or somebody else came in from the outside.'

'What we're saying amongst us is that these instructions to kill, we can't verify them. We can't go anywhere to verify them because we're under instructions to go dark.'

'We can verify them,' said Justin, 'with Anna.'

'What, just phone her and ask her?'

'I've known her long enough,' said Justin. 'I could tell from the response.'

'That's another gut feeling,' said Dom.

'We haven't got much else.'

'It's certainly something to put forward,' said Kirsten. 'I tried the work phone, it's not there. Not being taken and not been routed, but again, that makes sense if they think she's dirty. They've taken that off her. She is on the run, so call to one of the more private phones. Do you have a private line, Justin?'

'I've got a very private line. She'll pick up or at least she'll get back with a message.'

'Do it then,' said Kirsten, and Justin went to stand up and leave the room. 'No,' said Kirsten. 'Here. If she's on, I want to talk to her and I want everybody to hear what she says. I'm not just trusting your instinct. With all due respect, Justin, you're biased. You've worked with her for a long time. Dom and Carrie Anne are much fresher and much more removed from her.'

'Well, I can't really argue with that,' said Justin. He took out a mobile phone dialling in several numbers. 'It reaches through a different connection,' said Justin. 'It'll take a moment.' He placed the phone on the table, pressed the speaker button, and they listened waiting for the connection. It came through and began to ring. After five rings, it cut off on a voice message saying a message could be taken if required.

Dominic looked over at Kirsten. 'Just tell her to get in touch fast,' said Kirsten quietly, before letting Justin do just that.

After Justin had closed the call, Kirsten stood up pacing back and forward beside the table and then cleaned a whiteboard in the room with a cloth. She took out a pen and started writing up their options. She drew three columns. Column one; Anna was guilty as charged. The second column, Anna was innocent but had been involved in things that would mean that the search for her is justified. The third one, Anna was innocent and someone was out to get her.

'If we look at these,' said Kirsten, 'who are our enemies? If Anna is guilty, it's Anna. If Anna is innocent but they aren't following legitimate processes because of how things look, we don't have any enemies.'

'If Anna is being hunted down and innocent, everyone's our enemy.'

'How do you mean?' asked Kirsten.

'Anna could be our enemy if we're hunting her down. She's not going to react nicely if you stick a gun in her face. If we don't do as we're told, the rest of the agency will see us as outlaws if they know about it. The people who are putting us up to this all want to finish us off anyway. You're going to have to face it, boss, we're on our own.'

Kirsten looked over at Carrie Anne, and her analyst nodded. 'We're on our own. Dom is right. I suggest we play this by our rules though.'

'How do you mean?' asked Kirsten.

'The order is to kill Anna, so obviously, they want us to just find her, dispatch her. Don't even have to do it face to face, you could do it from a distance, I don't think they'd be bothered. However, that's not what we want to do. We want to get Anna, capture her, find out what's going on.'

'But there's another angle,' said Justin. 'She may be looking for help.'

'How so?' said Kirsten. 'She hasn't contacted any of us.'

'We haven't tried looking yet,' said Dom. 'She's not going to contact out of the blue like that. Not if she's on the run. She doesn't know they've got to you yet. She doesn't know where we stand. She's being careful. If a message comes, it will be simple. It'll be something you'll have to work to understand but also something that only we would understand.'

'The other problem is,' said Justin, 'if Anna is in trouble, they'll go after her connections.'

'What connections?' asked Kirsten. 'I don't think Anna has any.'

'She does. She's got a sister in Benbecula.'

'I didn't know that. She's in charge of me and I didn't know that. I'm meant to know the potential targets of influence for her,' said Kirsten. 'Why do I not know that?'

'Because the service doesn't know it either. Her sister had her name changed a long time ago. Anna is thorough, very thorough. Which is what really bothers me. You see, if she's on the run but she's keeping this low a profile, if she's innocent, this is something big.'

'Is there anything else you can think of, Justin?'

'There's two safe houses she might use because the agency doesn't know about them. She used them when I was working with her. Very low key. You'd struggle to recognise them as safe houses. She was very clever with them; they get rented out. People paying to occupy them who never came because it was Anna all the time. Somebody slushing money round and round but keeping that safe house available. Two of them. She told me about them because in one particular mission we were working on, she said if I had to run to get clear, I was to go to one of these two.'

'Who else knows about them?' asked Kirsten.

'Just me and Anna.'

Kirsten took a cloth and wiped clean the whiteboard she was writing on.

'We have to be very careful. We don't write anything down that we can't remove. We don't put anything in a computer system that we can't cover up. We act as if we're going for Anna, but our goal is to capture her and then find out what's going on.'

'And if she is dirty as they say she is?' asked Justin.

'Then we eliminate her, as we've been briefed,' said Kirsten. Dominic coughed and Carrie Anne looked with heavy eyes at Kirsten. 'I know. I don't like it any better than you do, but I want the proof.'

'And if they're after her?' asked Justin.

'Then all hell is breaking loose,' said Kirsten, 'because we'll have to work with her to change this. As it is, if we don't come back with anything, they'll not trust us again. So, given that we've got three places to cover, the first thing I'm going to do is send Dom over to Anna's sister in Benbecula. What's her name?' said Kirsten to Justin.

'She goes under Orla now, Orla O'Rourke, and she'll speak with an Irish accent. When you get close to her,' said Justin, 'call her Linda because that's her real name. It's only known by Anna and me.'

'Has she ever met you?' asked Kirsten.

'No,' said Justin. 'It wouldn't be any better sending me.'

'Fine. Dom goes to Benbecula, and we're going to the safe houses,' said Kirsten to Carrie Anne.

'They're North Berwick and Killen. Killen's a small village just north of Glasgow up in the hills.'

'Right,' said Kirsten, 'good. Justin, you're staying here because that's what you would do. In case anyone's got eyes on, keep a watch out. Report anybody that seems to be keeping tabs on what we're doing. If we need you, we'll call for you.'

'Should I work into the service? See if I can find anymore?'

'No,' said Kirsten. 'Leave it for the minute. You've gone looking for stuff, which is fair enough. You dig too much deeper and people realise, we'll seem like we're not following our orders. For now, we go to Benbecula and North Berwick. Let's find Anna and find out what the hell this is all about.'

Chapter 4

Kirsten and Carrie Anne set off at three in the morning for North Berwick while Dom went to sleep before catching the early flight via Stornoway to Benbecula. The islands were always more awkward to get to, but Kirsten didn't want to make any waves arriving in the dead of night on a charter. Instead, she booked Dom on the morning flight as just another visitor to the island.

The trip down to North Berwick was uneventful. As they passed through the mountains south of Inverness, Kirsten could see the snow lying on either side of the road. Soon, they would drop further down towards Perth and Edinburgh where the snow was gone. As the sun came through the sky, Kirsten could see the Forth Road Bridge approaching. She'd never been to North Berwick. She knew at times it could be quite a tourist attraction.

Given that they were now approaching Edinburgh just past seven o'clock, she reckoned by the time they reached North Berwick, it would be close to half-past eight. Kirsten justified a half-hour break for breakfast on the outskirts of Edinburgh before they continued on towards North Berwick. Carrie Anne was looking rather demure for her, again dressed in jeans and hiking boots with just a jumper on top. She was a classier dresser than Kirsten, and Kirsten knew she felt out of place when not wearing her finery, but the last thing she wanted to do in a tourist resort was to look like a tour guide or someone official.

The road into North Berwick became a tight affair, and as they strolled through the town, they realised it was quite difficult to navigate a one-way street down here, and with many people rushing out to their jobs, the traffic was reasonably heavy for such a small area. They passed the safe house, realising they couldn't stop on the street with the car, but Kirsten remembered a parking area she'd spotted close to the edge of the town and directed Carrie Anne towards it. When they arrived, Carrie Anne deposited several coins, allowing for a stay of over four hours before the women quietly set off together towards the house.

As they approached, Kirsten felt a chill in the air, the morning sun fighting to peer through a low cloud, and a light drizzle set in. The same chill was back in the mountains, but here, there was no snow around. For some reason, Kirsten thought it was almost colder because of it.

Carrie Anne approached the house from the front, knocking on the front door, while Kirsten searched around the rear. There were no signs of life from the building that sat in a row of houses along a tight street. The alley at the rear had a number of walls fencing off a backyard for each house. Kirsten jumped over the man-high wall, dropping into the courtyard behind. She tapped her earpiece, asking Carrie Anne if there was any response from the front, but she received a negative, and told Carrie Anne to remain in the street out front while Kirsten infiltrated the house.

Kirsten took out her lock picks and found the door opened quite easily. Thirty seconds later, she was opening the door when a voice came in her ear.

'Kilo. Someone about to enter. Stay back. I say again, stay back.'

'Roger.' Kirsten held back for a moment, but left the door unlocked, standing just on the other side of it.

'Figure is a male, approximately six foot two. No idea if armed.'

'Does he look like one of ours, Charlie?' asked Kirsten, using their call signs.

'Negative, Kilo, but looks like he's gone upstairs. If you're going to enter, now would be the time to do it.'

Kirsten opened the door, stepped quietly inside, and found herself in a small kitchen. There was a sink full of dishes, but Kirsten noted that there was mould growing on some of them. Whoever'd been here either hadn't done their dishes or hadn't been here for several days. She stepped quietly across the kitchen and pulled out her gun, holding it in front of her. She juked around the corner and then walked into the lounge, scanning the coffee table that sat in the middle. The carpet was cream, the walls that magnolia that goes on most new houses, and the sofa a blue colour that just did not fit. That was the thing about a safe house. You didn't decorate it to look good. You just put useful items of furniture inside.

'Is he still upstairs?' whispered Kirsten.

'Affirmative, Kilo.'

'Advise me if he—'

'No, he's not. He's not. I say again, I've lost him. I've lost him.'

Kirsten heard the click behind her head and raised her hands up to the sky. Her gun was taken away from her and thrown onto the floor. She heard the man stepping back away from her and then she was told to turn around. The man was indeed six foot two, wearing a balaclava now, but his eyes were looking intently at Kirsten.

'Are you here looking for her?' asked Kirsten.

'Quiet,' said the man.

'I don't think she's here. We could be on the same team.'

'I think not,' said the man, and now put a second hand up to his gun. Kirsten began to sweat. By the look of his eyes, he intended to shoot. She needed Carrie Anne and she needed her in a hurry.

As Kirsten began to tremble, aware that the man was pointing the gun simply at her head, she prayed for Carrie Anne to come in. Then she felt it, that slight draught. Maybe he did too because there was a moment's hesitation. Then there were two shots.

At the time, Kirsten could not distinguish one from the other. It was only afterwards she'd realised there were two. The first had been fired by Carrie Anne at some distance in the hall, but it was enough to tag the man on the shoulder. This, in turn, was enough to tear his arm to one side as he pulled the trigger, and the ceiling above Kirsten had a small hole dented in it. Both weapons were on silencers, but it still took Kirsten a moment to realise she hadn't been shot. The man, however, realised quickly he'd been hit, turned and ran through the kitchen and out the back.

Carrie Anne burst in, took a quick look at Kirsten. 'Are you okay?'

'Fine,' said Kirsten. 'Go.' Kirsten watched Carrie Anne race out of the kitchen. Then a voice came in her earpiece.

'He's gone out the rear. I think he's making towards the sea.'

'Follow him. I'm right behind you.'

Kirsten looked around the room, picked up her gun, put it in its holster, zipped her jacket, and begin to run out of the house, exiting by the rear door. When she got to the alleyway behind the house, she carefully closed the yard door behind her and began to sprint along the alleyway when she saw a couple of kids playing.

'They all ran that way,' said a little boy. 'Has he done something wrong?'

'We'll find out,' said Kirsten, and lifted her legs and began to run hard. She reached the end of the alleyway. It cut out across a road to a large area of green that ran along the shore. It was early morning and there were mainly dog walkers around with the occasional solo pedestrian. In the near distance, she could see Carrie Anne running hard. Kirsten put her head down and followed her.

The man cut this way and that before turning up towards the road that ran past the green area for a short distance. Kirsten could see Carrie Anne gaining on the man and she threw herself forward, wrapping her arms around his legs, knocking him over in a rugby tackle. There was a scuffle. Carrie Anne knocked him to the ground again before the man stood up, fighting back, holding her by the neck. As the two fought, Kirsten could see a car pull up along the road and a window was wound down. Even from the distance she was at, she could see the point of a gun.

'Carrie, down,' she shouted in her ear. 'Gun.'

In the next few seconds, a lot happened. First, Carrie Anne dropped to the ground. There was then a small flash from the muzzle of a silenced weapon sticking out of the car. Kirsten watched the man fall to the ground.

Without hesitating, Kirsten cut left and ran up an alleyway that led to the road that ran by the green. As she broke from the alleyway, she saw the dark red car that had been stopped with the weapon pointing out, and she stood in front of it, drawing her own weapon. It swerved this way and that, and she fired several times at it before the car just kept coming at her. As it got close, Kirsten moved onto the pavement, but the car mounted it, coming straight at her.

Beside her were metal railings, and then the green on the other side. Kirsten made a jump, grabbing the top of the railings and throwing herself over. The railings were then hit by the car, but it stayed on its own side. As Kirsten landed on the green and rolled up into a stance, she saw the car disappear off through the streets of North Berwick.

Kirsten tapped her earpiece. 'How's our man?'

'He's dead. Half his head's gone,' said Carrie Anne.

'Back to the house. Quick. Before anyone arrives, we need to do a quick search and go.'

Kirsten set the timer on her stopwatch and began to run back to the house. She cut back to the alley and as she ran past the little boy, she turned round and handed him a pound coin.

'Go and get yourself an ice cream or something,' she said.

'Mum doesn't let me have ice cream.'

'It's obviously not a school day. Go for it.' She watched him run off. It wasn't the best cover, but at least he'd be out of the way if the police came around. As she reached the back door of the house, she could hear sirens and she enquired on Carrie Anne's status.

'In the alley, coming on up behind you. Just start the search. I'll be there very shortly.'

'We need to get out of here,' said Carrie Anne as she came into the house.

'No,' said Kirsten, 'we don't. We need to search the house quickly. Then we need to get somewhere we can watch.'

'How so?' asked Carrie Anne as she began to rifle through some books on a shelf in the living room.

'If nobody knows about this place, I want to see who comes for a look. I want to see who cleans up this mess. There's just been a shooting in public in North Berwick. That doesn't happen very often. I want to see if it's the normal police or if some other people make an appearance.'

'Good thinking,' said Carrie Anne. 'I'll take upstairs then.' And she broke off from the book she was looking at and climbed the stairs of the house. Kirsten looked around. Well, she thought, we'd better get on with this quick. There's a whole house to cover and all sorts of trouble charging into North Berwick.

Chapter 5

Kirsten kept one eye on the window as she made her way around the living room, searching here, there, and everywhere. She was checking on the plant pots, inside of cabinets, behind curtains, anywhere she could possibly think something could be left. There was little that appeared to be Anna's. A few magazines lay around, but she never saw Anna as the crocheting type.

Kirsten could hear Carrie Anne above her, going through bedrooms. Within five minutes, they'd searched the entire place. They had done a quick search, for it had to be, as they didn't know if anyone was going to be coming back to the house. Surely, people would have seen the man running, but would they have clocked where he'd come from? Maybe the boy that she'd sent off with the money, but hopefully he would have been distracted enough that the police wouldn't find him for a while.

Carrie Anne came down the stairs, shaking her head. 'There's nothing up there,' she said, 'I've got nothing. There aren't any clothes, nothing. This place is barely lived in at all.'

'Well, she must check in every once in a while. There's no damp. It's aired. I'm nearly done. I'm just going through the sofa,' said Kirsten.

Carrie Anne took the other end. As they lifted up cushions, they found nothing in the sofa, underneath the cushions, or underneath the larger cushions that made up the seats. Kirsten knelt down on the floor and tilted the seat back up, Carrie Anne catching it as the weight of its topside made it topple over.

'Well, that's different,' said Kirsten. She saw a yellow post-it note on the underside of the sofa.

'What have we got?' asked Carrie Anne.

'Well, it's a post-it note. It just says, "Walter".'

'Walter? Never heard of a Walter.'

'Me neither, but maybe it means something to Justin. Anyway, let's get out of here in case the police show up.'

'You want to head back up the road?' asked Carrie Anne.

'No,' said Kirsten, 'we're staying in North Berwick for a while. I want to see if anyone comes here.'

The pair retreated for the alley, making their way out through the kitchen and the yard, but then turning away from the green, going into the centre of the town. They made their way back around to the car where they deposited their weapons, aware that there'd be a lot more police around. They didn't want to explain why they were carrying them.

On return to the street where the house was located, Kirsten spotted a small coffee shop, and directed Carrie Anne towards it. Together they sat down in the window seat, ordered a coffee and cake, and generally sat back and relaxed for a while. Kirsten let her hair hang forward, no longer tied up behind her, shielding her face from many of the onlookers as they gazed in the window.

Her eyes were focused on the house across. She saw police

cars race down, local pedestrians becoming agitated. As people began to band together to discuss what was happening, she saw the shock wave that went through the place as the road was closed much further up and the rumours started filtering into the cafe of the man who had been shot dead. Carrie Anne had been fortunate. She had dropped to the ground with the man standing just behind her. When he'd been hit, he'd been thrown backwards. Most of his head had ended up on the green lawn behind her. She looked a little dishevelled. Other than that, she was fine, slight marks around her trousers, easily passed off due to their supposed hiking activities that morning.

Kirsten watched the police comb along the street. They started stopping people and asking them if they had heard anything, or had they seen anything regarding the shooting? One young officer entered the coffee house and went over to speak to Carrie Anne and Kirsten. But they shook their heads, putting on a face of horror at what had happened. It wasn't difficult, despite the work that they did. It was the sort of brutality done to a body that still made them sick to the core.

Kirsten saw a man on the far side of the street that she thought she recognised. As he came closer, she saw the thick neck, the chiselled chin. It was Craig, her man from London. He was dressed in a pair of jeans with a jumper on and a bag over his shoulder. He walked up to the house Carrie Anne and Kirsten had searched, stood at the door, cleverly disguising one hand working with the lock. Kirsten watched as his eyes swept up and then down the street to make sure he wasn't being observed, but she had him.

'That's the—'

'Yes,' said Kirsten, 'that's the driver from London.'

'Do you think he followed us?'

'I didn't see anyone tail us, did you?'

'No, I didn't. Do you think he tapped into the satellite from above? The question is who is he working for and why?' asked Carrie Anne.

'I've a good mind to go over and ask him,' said Kirsten.

'You're having a laugh, aren't you?'

'No, I'm not.' Kirsten's face was full of rage and Carrie Anne was clocking it.

'What's up? How do you know him?'

'He's the driver from London,' said Kirsten.

'No,' said Carrie Anne. 'How do you really know him?'

Kirsten almost swore under her breath, but it wasn't Carrie Anne's fault. She was looking out for herself and the team.

'Last week when I was away, I shared his bed,' said Kirsten.

'You know him that well. What's he doing here then? Why didn't you say so when you were down in London?'

'No one's supposed to know,' said Kirsten. 'We met the first time I went down to London, and he drove me to meet Control at that point. We had time to kill before my plane back up north. I asked him to take me to a coffee shop and we got talking, talking about things not related to the job, dreams and plans, and that. You need someone in this job, Carrie Anne, don't you? Someone not in the job, someone who can give you that normality of life, the things that, well, everybody wants.'

'Closeness,' said Carrie Anne; 'you're talking about closeness, aren't you, not just sex?'

'No, not just that but closeness. You're right. But what's he doing following me? Why hasn't he told me?'

'Well, you said you were keeping it separate. You didn't acknowledge him. He's not acknowledging you. Maybe he has good reason to follow you up. Maybe people are worried about us.'

'You don't really believe that, do you?' asked Kirsten. She saw Craig exiting the house. 'I have a good mind to run down that street and get a hold of him.'

'How do you know he's not being watched?' asked Carrie Anne. 'You need to leave it.'

'If he's tailing me now . . . then maybe the other week. We don't know how long Anna's been involved with this.'

'What, do you think he took you to bed to get details from you? Did it feel like that?'

'Of course, it didn't feel like that,' said Kirsten. 'If it did, I would've walked. I'm not that needy.'

'Lucky you,' said Carrie Anne, and almost instantly regretted the throw-away comment.

'Who?' said Kirsten. Then she stopped herself. 'No, don't tell me. I don't need to know. If it doesn't interfere with work, I don't need to know.'

'Good,' said Carrie Anne, 'because I wouldn't tell you. More to the point. What are we going to do about this? How do you think they followed us? There's two people connected with that house. The man who's now lying dead on the green and your man. I don't understand. Who are they working for? Why would they know about the safe houses? Justin said that only he and Anna knew about them.'

'Apparently not,' said Kirsten. 'Somebody else clearly knew.'

Carrie Anne watched Kirsten's face. 'You seem to have some wrinkle lines there,' she said. 'What's the matter?'

'Well, think about it. If they've come here, if they've known about this safe house, what's to stop them knowing about the next safe house? What's stopping them knowing about her sister?'

'You think Dom could be in trouble? He should be over there by now.'

'I'll give him a call. Let him know he may be being watched.' Kirsten picked up her phone and let it ring until Dom answered and then advised him briefly of the situation.

'I'm only here. Haven't seen anything yet. I'm going to watch the house for the day. Once I've done that, I might have a look at night. Maybe speak to her about getting her out. I need to see the lay of the land first. The moment I take her away, she becomes no one. People will miss her,' said Dom. 'Therefore, I have to make sure when I go, I'm going and leaving no trace behind.'

'Just be aware, Dom, not to take too long. There could be other people on our tail. We don't know.' Kirsten closed off the call and then placed a call to Justin Chivers, relaying the events of the day.

'Yes, it's all over the news. Man with his head half shot off. North Berwick. Says it's not linking it to anything. Possibly a drug incident.'

'Anything else come out? Not in the media, but through the service.'

'Nothing so far,' said Justin. 'I'm looking into it, but it's very quiet. I thought there would be a bigger response on this. It's like somebody has quashed it and said this is drug related and nothing to do with the service. And yet, it's quite clear that this guy was an agent of some sort.'

'I don't like it,' said Kirsten. 'I really don't. I'm worried. We're being hung out to dry here. Possibly we're being tailed, and we've got Dom on his own over in Benbecula.'

'Dom can handle himself,' said Carrie Anne, interrupting the phone call. 'It's Dom.'

'She's right,' said Justin on the phone. 'He's an old hand. He'll play it cool.'

The two women finished their coffee and made their way back to the car. They couldn't sit there all day. For the rest of it, they took turns in walking across the street, checking to see if anyone was at the house or in the entry, but the police never came to the house specifically. The only person to have entered the house other than the dead man was Craig, and it was gnawing at Kirsten just why he did it.

Chapter 6

om sat watching from the croft land at the rear of Orla O'Rourke's house. He had asked briefly where the house was, stopping at a small shop. His choices to hire a car were not great, but he managed to acquire one and had left it half a mile behind at the side of the road. Lying down in the moorland, he watched with binoculars as a small woman with blonde hair strolled out to hang up her washing. He could see why she was Anna's sister.

Despite being small, she had an elegance to her and a determination in the face. It was not a perfect face and even at this distance with the binoculars, Dom could see how time had aged it, but doubtless she'd lived. Maybe she had as interesting a past as Anna. Who knew? What Dom did know was that the woman could be in real trouble. On the bright side, anyone approaching the house would be seen from quite a distance. Maybe that was why she bought this one. Maybe she simply decided to live without fear, or maybe Anna had advised it.

When Dom had taken the call from Kirsten, he'd become more worried and decided instead of going into the village to find out more about Orla O'Rourke, he would instead watch the house in case of anyone coming for her. He wouldn't approach it until that night, moving under cover of darkness so no one would see him.

He was thankful for the sandwiches he had purchased at the shop, devouring them greedily and ignoring the wind whipping across his back. *Always wind in these islands,* he thought; *windy, often wet, chilly to the bone.* He lay down again, binoculars trained on the house and watched the woman carry the empty washing basket inside. *She looked good for her years,* he thought, knowing he was not that young.

It had been bugging him lately. When was he getting out of the scheme? When was he going to settle down? When would he-—what? Start up a family? He couldn't, could he? He shouldn't, and yet Dom wanted someone to pass things on to. He spent his life alone. Yes, there'd been women. Of course, there had. Too many of them were short affairs, nothing but carnal releases, even the woman at the moment . . . and he stopped, thinking about her for a second.

She had saved his life, he thought. She'd been there when Dom had been shot and saved his life. In some ways, Carrie Anne had come like a bolt out of the blue when he got assigned to the team in Inverness. After the incident, they'd hit it off. She'd been there for his recovery, the time it had taken when he had no one else. Sure, Kirsten and Justin were good colleagues visiting him, but Carrie Anne had sat at the times when he felt low and then made- . . . well, they just got together. Neither of them agreed what it was. It just was. The only thing they had agreed was that they weren't going to tell anyone else.

You shouldn't do it anyway, Dom thought. You shouldn't keep that sort of thing going within your own team, but what the hell, he wasn't getting any younger and in truth, Carrie

Anne wasn't either. Maybe they both needed someone to find. He shook his head, instead trying to think about the horse racing, or the football, or anything else because the more he thought about Carrie Anne, the colder he felt. It'd be a long wait until nightfall, and it was better filled with idle thoughts rather than longing ones.

* * *

Dom could see the last aircraft take off from the airport, also, on the west side of Benbecula but further north of his current location. The night sky was cloudy, and as he watched the aeroplane depart, he realised that the cloud base must be a good four or five thousand feet. However, the night still had the stars and his approach to the house would be easy.

There was a light on. Orla O'Rourke was still up, and he began to make his way across the croft land, stepping over the odd barbed wire fence that segregated the long crofts from each other. Under foot, the ground was soft due to recent rain and snow, but Dom had been lying on it all day and the cold had already penetrated to his bones. He couldn't get any colder, and all thoughts of discomfort were pushed far to the back of his mind. He needed to go in, convince Anna's sister of the plight she was in, get into her car, and drive away.

Maybe he would take her to an abandoned house he'd seen over six miles away to the northeast. From there, he would contact Kirsten and they would get Orla off the island. Of course, Dom would speak to her in that time first, find out more about her sister, see if Orla could shed any light on what Anna was doing.

Dom counted the fences in front of him, another two, and

he trudged on across the moorland. He was dressed in black. It wasn't that hard to see but still he felt every movement of his muscles as he swung himself over the next fence. The wind whipped at his chin, and he swore if he could feel it, it would still be cold.

As he got close to the house, a set of headlights appeared on the road in the distance. Dom quietly knelt down, not bothered by this because he expected the road to have cars on it. They came every now and again. It was no issue to him, but then he watched this one turn and follow the path that led to the house.

He lay down on the sodden ground as the car headlights swept across the top of him and the car pulled up beside the house. From his position, Dom could see feet on the far side of the car, and those feet were joined by Orla O'Rourke as she stepped out of the front door of her house. A light was shining above her, and Dom could see the blonde hair being whipped to one side.

A man joined her, embraced her and they kissed longingly before almost falling inside the house. Dom heard the door slam shut and was back up on his feet again, quickly jumping over the next fence before making his way onto the path of the house.

He approached the rear door, looking in and seeing that the hall light was on, but he saw no one there. He snuck around the side of the house peering up into the kitchen where again the light was on, but no one was in. As he rounded the house and came to the large front window, the room lights were off, but a fire had cast an orange glow across it allowing him to see that no one was in the room.

Dom made his way back to the rear of the house, carefully

opened the back door, and stepped inside. He listened, eager for any signs to identify just where the couple had gone. There was a thumping from up the stairs and he slowly climbed them before peering around at the top. He saw a half open door and a pair of buttocks moving up and down. There were little yells and squeals and Dom wondered if this was the moment to step in.

It would be better if the man left, allowing Dom to take Orla away on his own. He didn't want any trouble, didn't want to have to knock the man out or to leave him somewhere, but he had a job to do. As he stood on the stairs, Dom heard the pair come to the finish and then breathlessly talk to each other. The man would be going in an hour, apparently for he had work tomorrow. Besides, his wife couldn't find out.

All the more reason, Dom thought, *to let the man go*. That would just bring difficulties and the wife being irate, maybe the police being involved, things getting unravelled, instead of a simple disappearance by a single woman. Dom made his way back downstairs and took up a position at the rear of the hall.

He put his hand through the various coats that were hanging under the stairs, eager to find if there was any information about Anna in the house. He then made his way into the living room, but there were no photos of Anna Hunt. There were hardly any photos at all. He made his way into the kitchen, saw the water and was almost desperate for a drink, but he couldn't do it, not until he confronted her.

Dom could hear movement up above and believed the man would be departing soon, so he exited from the rear of the house and made his way out into the croft land again, getting down low. The wind was whipping hard, and Dom was struggling to hear anything from the house, but when the front light came on, he smiled realising that this evening was about to come to a quick close. However, the couple stood there in the front door light, kissing away as if they hadn't seen each other for the past hour and a half. All Dom could think was, *Hurry up. Come on. Let's go*, but instead, he had to endure the prolonged departing.

Then he heard a sound over the wind. It was difficult to pick out. Then he realised it was a car . . . no, louder than a car. He turned his eyes down the path out to the road and swore he saw a vehicle moving through the shadows. There were no lights illuminated on it.

As it drove up, Dom could see the couple suddenly realise they weren't alone. The van doors opened, and men jumped out shouting at them. Dom could see weapons, or at least the outline of them, and he moved quickly through the grass and moss, getting himself to the nearby fence and throwing himself over before bending down again.

The men with the weapons started to push the couple inside and soon the front door light went out. Dom looked over at the van, wondering if there was anybody still inside. Then he crawled his way to a view of the front door. He stole his way around to the rear and realised that the kitchen light had gone out, as had that of the hall. Very clever, he thought, making sure they weren't seen from the road.

Dom snuck slowly up to the hallway door, cracked open the back door of the house that led to the hallway and leaned up against it listening. He could hear voices shouting roughly. A woman screamed. He thought he heard the sickening thud of a rifle butt driven at someone's head.

Against every instinct, he held back, knowing that if he

entered not knowing the lay of the land, he could easily get taken out by someone he didn't clock quick enough. He'd have to do this slowly, wait for them. He made his way around the side of the house, making sure the van was still sitting there and listened down at the wall. It seemed they were all in the front room, or at least those who were talking.

Dom didn't dare sneak around the front to get a look. He knelt down by the wall, pulled out his weapon and decided he needed to sit this out, wait until there was an angle where he could see everyone, know what he was up against. If only he hadn't been alone, he could go in and have backup, someone like Carrie Anne.

She always came to his rescue, didn't she? He stopped himself. Maybe it was because he was cold, maybe it was because he was alone, but he didn't have time for thoughts like that. He needed to end this situation soon. Then Dom heard movement from inside the house.

The front door was thrown open. He peered round and saw Orla O'Rourke with a bag over her head being dragged towards the van. It was going to be now or never. He felt the chill in his bones. How many of them were there? He thought at least four. How many were in the van? Dom swallowed hard. *Pick your moment. Pick your moment, Dom, son,* he said to himself.

Chapter 7

om watched as some of the attackers started gesticulating to each other. Clearly, they weren't happy about being at the front of the house. Some pointed to the road and to a light above their heads. Dom wondered if he should take a shot now, but again, he was worried about the consequences. He didn't have the ability to fire all around him. He was quick with a weapon but not that quick, especially when he hadn't identified exactly how many people were there. If more came from the van, he'd be outflanked, outnumbered, and probably dead.

His key objective was Anna's sister, but he couldn't simply save Orla and let the other man die. As far as Dom could make out, the man was innocent, a bystander. That wasn't something you let happen.

He watched pensively from his position until he saw a man who seemed like the one in charge indicate that they should drag the man round to the rear of the house. Dom watched him being picked up. He thought he could charge the van getting Orla out from inside it, but as he thought about making this manoeuvre, Orla was dragged back out of the van.

Then everyone was taken to the back of the house. Dom spun round his side of the house being able to view the rear where he fought to see through what little light there was. Orla's lover was put on his knees and a gun now put to his head. Orla was brought beside him, the hood pulled off her head, and a hand covered over her mouth as she went to scream.

'Make a sound and he dies right now.'

Dom watched Orla fighting through tears as her body shook with terror. The man behind her slowly let his hand off her mouth but kept a firm arm around her throat.

'Your sister. Where is your sister?'

'I don't have a sister.'

'You know who I mean. Your sister, Anna. Where is Anna?'

Dom listened to the accent, and he thought at first it was Russian, but some things didn't make sense. Why would the Russians be coming after Anna's sister if Anna was meant to be a mole? Secondly, that accent wasn't holding up. The more the man spoke, the more Dom could see the inflections were not correct. The accents dropped here and there.

'I asked you before, where is Anna? Tell me.'

Orla shook her head, crying hard, but the man behind her grabbed her blonde hair pulling it backwards, forcing Orla to look at her lover beside her. The man couldn't see a thing. He still had a hood over his head. Then the man in charge stepped up in front of him and smashed the gun butt into his face. Dom heard the man cry out and then he began to weep underneath that hood.

'She doesn't have a sister. She lives alone here,' said a voice from under the hood. The gun butt was smacked into the man's forehead again and Dom wondered if he'd have to step in quickly. He tried to pick out the figures around the back of the house. He counted one, two, three. There was another one at a distance. How many in the van? He spun round up the side of the house and looked round the front, but the van was in darkness.

Should he go to it? Should he try and take out whoever was in there? It was a short distance to run in front of the house but the light was still on. It wouldn't look unusual to anyone coming along the road, but it also meant he'd have to cross in front of the light towards the van and he felt that if anyone was inside watching, he'd be dead before he got four feet.

Dom spun back around, peered round the edge of the house to look at the rear of it.

'I'll ask you one more time and if you don't answer, I'll blow his head off,' said the man. 'If you want, I'll let you watch him.' The man stepped forward and pulled the hood up and Dom could see the bloody mess that was the face of Orla's lover. Orla was freaking out, fighting to hold back her tears, but the moments when she did cry out, the man behind her slapped her on the face telling her to be quiet, to focus, to tell his boss where Anna was. Once again Dom was left to rue the fact he was on his own.

'You're leaving me no choice,' said the man, and raised a gun with a silencer on it to the forehead of Orla's lover. Dom saw the man shake and from the distance he was at he began to smell the pungent aroma of the man wetting himself. *There's nothing civilized in this. It was all brutal, highly brutal, and also somewhat over the top,* thought Dom. *Why would you do this here? Why not bring the man along?*

'One more time I ask you,' said the leader. 'One more time.' Once again, the butt of his gun drove into the face of the lover.

'I don't know who you're talking about.' The leader put the gun in front of the lover's face.

'Okay, okay,' said Orla, bending forward and beginning to

weep again. 'I told you before I have no sister but that's a lie. Anna hasn't been here. Why do you want Anna? I haven't seen Anna in months. This is the last place she would come. Anna wouldn't do this.'

Dom tried to understand what was going on. They were looking for where Anna was, but if Anna was on the run, there's no way she'd tell her sister where she was going, and this felt so amateur. You would drag them away, take them somewhere, but then again, maybe they had nowhere to operate out of. He found that hard to believe that if they were Russian agents that they couldn't have found a base. Or was it somebody playing at being Russian agents?

He thought of the accent. Maybe that made sense. It was becoming hard to know who to trust. Not just in the sense of actually trusting them, but of actually trusting what they were doing. Was everything he was looking at real?

'Okay,' said the man, 'this is the last time I ask you. Where is Anna?' Orla, in tears, knelt forward, her face looking at the ground till the man behind her grabbed her blonde hair again, pulling her hair backwards forcing her to look at the leader of the men.

'I told you, I don't know. Even if you kill him, I won't know. I just don't know.'

Dom raised his weapon confident it wouldn't shine in any moonlight so cloudy was the night, but he had a problem because the outline of the leader wasn't that great either.

'Have it your way then,' said the leader, and raised the weapon almost casually with one arm. Dom didn't hesitate and fired. The distance was reasonable and with the darkness it was hard to pick the exact target on the man, but Dom saw him spin. The others began to raise weapons wondering at first where the shot had come from. Dom took another shot but seemed to disappear off into the distance. His weapon was silenced but he was sure that they must have seen some sort of flash come out of the muzzle, especially in this darkness.

Dom stepped forward from his position and in the darkness saw Orla being pulled away screaming, dragged by her hair backwards. The leader of the men seemed to pick himself up, stumbling along, apparently without a weapon. Dom raced forward to Orla's lover, standing beside him, eager to shoot at anyone who looked to shoot back. With one hand, he grabbed him by the collar dragging him back toward his side of the house, aware that the others were now vacating to the other side of the house and towards the van.

Once Dom had dragged the man clear of the rear of the house, he let him go and spun round looking out towards the van at the front. Dom could see Orla being put into the van and he immediately put a shot up taking out the light at the front of the house. There were cries and Dom shouted from his position before running off into the darkness and shouting again, crying out that the people were surrounded. The van began to move but Dom could see, with the changes of the shades of black, that a few of the men were still running to get inside.

He fired again and again, careful to aim at the front cab and not into the rear in case he would hit Orla. He stepped forward trying to get closer, fired at the tyres and heard one burst. They couldn't get far if he kept doing that, but he saw the van begin to turn around and then make its way out to the road. Dom shot again hitting the rear of the van at least another two times and continued to shout loudly. As he got to the end of the track that led down to the house, Dom realised that the van was still moving well despite having one tyre partially blown out. Wherever he hit it, it must have had some air still in it and they'd be able to get away.

Dom routed back and found the man he had left behind still at the side of the house, moaning. Dom reached inside his pocket, pulled out a torch, shone it on the man's face. He was a mess, bleeding profusely, but before Dom grabbed him, he made his way round to the rear of the house, located the weapon that had fallen from the leader's hands and also saw where some blood had spilled from where he'd managed to hit the leader.

It must have been on the shoulder or arm. Dom cursed his bad luck. If he'd taken it in the head, he might have caused a lot more confusion. Dom gathered the weapon and made his way back to the fallen lover, put the man's arm around his own neck, picked him up and carried him out towards the main road. He left him there before running off to find his car and bringing it back.

Dom looked up his phone, searching for a hospital in the area and he saw what he thought must be a small cottage hospital. Certainly nothing as big as you would get on the mainland. He'd have to go there as the man was in quite a state.

Dom picked him up, put him into the front seat, jumped in the car, and drove quickly along the roads. The small hospital was in a reasonably built-up area and Dom decided he couldn't be spotted. The team was meant to be dark at the moment, investigating, and so Dom pulled into the carpark, stopped, looked around and saw no one there. There were lights on in the hospital, probably the night shift looking after what few patients were there.

Dom stepped out of the car, made his way around, opened

the passenger side door, and put his arms underneath the man who was barely murmuring. Dom pulled him to the front door. Then he banged loudly shouting for assistance. He saw a nurse coming towards the door in the distance and Dom turned and got into the car. As soon as he saw the doors of the hospital open, Dom drove off as quickly as he could.

He'd have to burn the car or he'd need to hire another or steal one. The man's blood was in the car. It would be difficult to explain and certainly he couldn't do it without revealing himself to some degree. Dom drove away, making his way out of Benbecula and up towards North Uist. He drove off into the middle of nowhere parking the car up below a small track.

He had seen a house not that far back with what looked like a tractor. He'd find his way back there, see if he could find some diesel. It would usually be stored separately in containers and Dom would steal some, come back, and burn the car.

He picked up his phone. He needed to talk to Kirsten, find out what to do next, but he noticed that there was no signal. *Blast these islands*, he thought. *Right when you need something.*

Slowly Dom made his way back out to the track, following it back to the house he had seen and feeling the cold of the wind. His mission had been to get to Orla, to bring her away. Somebody else had her. Who are they? Why do they want her? The Russians couldn't be looking for Anna, could they? If it wasn't treason as he suspected, who were these people, and how desperate were they to find her?

Dom sucked in as much air as possible as he walked, trying to rejuvenate himself, but it seemed that these days, as he got older, anything worked after the midnight hour just seemed to feel a little sore around his bones.

Chapter 8

Kirsten turned over in her bed. They had travelled back to the outskirts of Edinburgh, stopping at a cheap hotel for the night. She tossed and turned, Anna on her mind, until a phone call from Dom had woken her properly. It was three in the morning, and he sounded rattled as he debriefed Kirsten on what had occurred. Her heart began to sink, and she wondered exactly where Anna's sister was, fearing greatly for the woman. Kirsten wasn't sold yet that Anna was a traitor, and if she wasn't, the last thing she'd want for anyone was for one of their siblings to be taken out.

Dom had made his way to a small farmhouse and stolen some fuel and was about to burn the car he had been driving around in, but he knew that once he did set fire to it, he'd have to get out of the area quickly.

'I'm feeling very under-resourced at the moment, to be honest, boss,' said Dom. 'I can't really go back to the hire company and there isn't that many here. In fact, I think there's only one. I can't exactly pitch up to hire another one, having burnt out their last one. I have to burn it out. The man's blood is all over the front seat.'

'You're doing the right thing, Dom,' said Kirsten. 'I'm going to come over and we'll get on the trail of these gunmen. I think we'll send Carrie Anne off down to the safe house in Killen.'

'You think that's wise? You need to send people in with backup at the moment, Kirsten. I needed it here.'

'I understand that, but I needed it up here as well, Dom. If Carrie Anne hadn't been here, I could have been in serious trouble.'

'Then I suggest you get Justin off his arse and out onto the streets with us.'

'I'd rather have him running a central communication. That makes more sense. You take that away from him if you make him go out in the field.'

'I appreciate that,' said Dom, 'but at the moment we've been told to go dark. You've been told to use your unit. That is us. You, me, Carrie Anne, Justin. The man knows what to do in the field.'

Kirsten thought for a moment. The advantage of Justin still being at the office was he could infiltrate the service. He had contacts, ways of getting in touch which he'd lose if he came away, if people thought he was out there as well. Could he be as secure working through the internet? It didn't matter. She needed to protect her team. She needed someone with Carrie Anne. Dom was right.

'Okay, Dom. That's settled. I'm going to get in the car and drive to the ferry. I'll be over with you in the morning. Get that car alight, get clear. I'll meet you down at Lochmaddy. Be looking for me coming off the ferry. Carrie Anne can pick up another car here and meet Justin down in Killen. I'll get on to him now, but you do what you have to do, then get clear. Keep your head down.'

'Do you think they'll leave though? I mean with Orla?' asked Dom.

'Well, to be honest, they have to get the information out of her, or she's no longer an asset, and get rid of her. But they'll sit with her, hold onto her. Even if she doesn't say anything, even if she doesn't know anything, if they want Anna, she could always be a factor. They could always play her. Say they're going to kill her sister unless Anna comes out of the woodwork. Last thing I would do is give her up. If you're right there in the isles, it's a good place to hide. Not a lot of eyes about, especially if you go somewhere quiet.'

'Good point,' said Dom. 'Try and bring some food with you when you come over. I doubt I'm going to get anything. Probably best if I don't show my face. Let you do all the contact work once you get here.'

'Good idea, especially because they'll be looking for whoever rented that car.'

Kirsten closed down the call and spun out of bed. She looked at her watch, then got hold of her laptop, finding out when the ferry would next leave Uig on Skye, to go over to Lochmaddy on North Uist. North Uist was attached to Benbecula and was one of three islands set from north to south with South Uist at the bottom. The ferry was leaving at eight o'clock, so Kirsten would need to drive quickly. When she banged Carrie Anne's door, the woman made her way through into Kirsten's room, sitting down on the bed, watching while Kirsten was packing quickly.

'I'm going to contact Justin,' said Kirsten, 'get him to go with you to Killen. Dom's had trouble over there. I need to get to him.'

'Okay,' said Carrie Anne. 'You are taking our operative away from the base though. He might not be able—'

'That's fine,' said Kirsten. 'I've thought this through. Okay?'

'Okay, boss,' said Carrie Anne. 'I just need to remind you of it. It's my job.'

'I know. I'm sorry. I'm a little bit tense. Dom's out in the open at the moment. I want to get him secure, and I want to get to Anna's sister.'

'Keep your options open,' said Carrie Anne. 'I find it hard to believe that Anna is a traitor either, but you have to be open to the possibility. You have to be open to everything.'

'Spoken like a true analyst,' said Kirsten.

'Of course. So, don't put your eggs in any baskets. Trust very few people. I'll get off around about six, meet up with Justin. He's coming down from Inverness. By the time he gets down towards Glasgow to head up north, you'll probably be going over on the ferry.'

'Just watch your back. Dom had people come for Orla. I had Craig, the driver, turn up in North Berwick. We had the other man in there who was shot by another party. I'm not sure who's after who here or what's going on. What I do know is that we keep getting caught in the middle.'

'It's okay,' said Carrie Anne. 'I know how to look after myself. So does Justin. You just be careful. You're out of reach of help when you go to the islands. Be aware of that.'

Kirsten shook Carrie Anne's hand before departing. Dressed now in her black jeans and black t-shirt, she stopped outside the hotel she was staying in and pulled into a garage, filling her car up with petrol. She took a large coffee, realising she was going to be up through the night, and grabbed a sandwich, throwing it on the seat of the car. She pulled out onto the motorway at the south of Edinburgh, preparing to head back up north, but as she drove, she put a call in to Justin.

'What's the crisis?' asked a voice at the other end. 'Have you found her?'

'No,' said Kirsten. 'Dom's had trouble. I'm routing over to the Benbecula to be with him. We've lost Anna's sister. She's been taken by another group.' Kirsten laid out the full detail of what happened to Dom. 'Did you get any luck from earlier on?' asked Kirsten. After the incident in North Berwick, Kirsten had advised Justin of the post-it note they'd found and the words, 'Walter.'

'Mulling over it, going through contacts of Anna, there's no Walter within her service life, no code word Walter, anything like that, but I did hear her mention Walter before. It was in the context of her sister, so I think she's met him. If we can get the sister, we may find out where Walter is,' said Justin.

'Great,' said Kirsten. 'Just great. The one person that can get us on anywhere and she's been taken by who knows who. Okay, don't let me keep you back; you've got an early start. I want you down with Carrie Anne. Give her a call and arrange your rendezvous. Get up to Killen and see if you can find anything else. And Justin?'

'Yes, boss.'

'Be careful. Watch each other's back. I mightn't have been about here except for Carrie Anne, and Dom's had enough trouble on his own. From now on, we stay in pairs everywhere you go. I don't like this. It feels like—'

'It feels like we're being used,' said Justin. 'Why would you send someone's own team after them? I mean, Anna practically set you up. In some ways, you're Anna's go-to girl. Why would they send you after her?'

'They said because I know her.'

'That's the exact reason why I wouldn't send you after her.'

'Then, you think there's a game being played here?'

'It's the Secret Service. It's Anna. It's talk of a traitor, it's talk of information to Russia. Of course, there's a game being played. If Control is from a different service, it could be even worse. You've got to be careful on this one, Kirsten. This isn't like our normal operations. It isn't like when we charge after a terrorist, or we go infiltrating with the cavalry waiting to charge in behind us. When we find out what's going on here, we might not like it and you might have some very difficult decisions about what to do.'

'I get you, Justin, I really do, but you need to get your backside down here.'

'Okay,' said Justin, 'but go find her sister. Walter was a good friend if I remember right. A number of times when she talked about when they were younger, Walter was mentioned. She'd used to tell me about Walter being there or something. Anna, Linda, and Walter.'

'Okay, Justin, I get the message.' She closed down the call. Kirsten stared into the night, watching the car headlights coming along the motorway on the far side. It was quiet with not many about. Then Kirsten watched to see if anyone was tailing her. The only thing she was unhappy about at the moment was leaving Carrie Anne on her own. She was going to get the boat to get over to Dom; she'd be required. The other difficulty was keeping Dom incognito while searching. When Kirsten got there, they'd have to change his appearance, do something about that. He couldn't just walk around like he had before.

It wasn't long before she broke off the motorway and started heading up to the northwest, making her way up towards Skye.

As she got closer, she began to see the snow drifting down. There had been a forecast saying it was coming but it would only be light. As Kirsten continued to drive further in the flurries, she realised that this was heavy. It wasn't uncommon for the forecast to get it wrong, and she wondered what the island would be like when she got there. It was now past seven, light was beginning to dawn, and she could see that the flakes were lying all around.

The road out to Uig on the Isle of Skye was a bending, twisting one. It took her eventually out to Portree with its winding, narrow streets. They looked beautiful covered in white. She made another stop at a co-op to pick up sandwiches and drinks before racing away further around the long road out to Uig. On either side, she saw the moorland now covered white.

When she reached the bay, she could see the ferry docked in front of her. She had about an hour and a half to kill alongside the ferry, but then she drove the car on board. She looked around her, seeing if she could see any faces she should know. Had anyone been following her? She thought not. She took up a position in the café and sat watching the other passengers. If she saw them on the island close to her, she would know something was up. She connected with Dom on the mobile phone, and she could hear him shivering.

'Where did this come from? It's white everywhere here.'

'Have you not managed to find yourself some shelter?'

'I am. I'm stuck in an old rundown house in Lochmaddy.'

'I should be there in an hour and a half. Don't come to the ferry terminal. I'll pick you up on the road just out from it.'

'There's a community play park in Lochmaddy, head for it,' said Dom. 'I'm able to get some shelter close by. Just stop, I'll approach the car and get in. From there we can start making our way about.'

'Good,' said Kirsten. 'You be ready for granddad protocol.'

'You've got to be joking,' said Dom.

'No, you've been seen. Granddad protocol it is. Besides, with how cold it's been, I bet your joints are feeling that at the moment.'

Kirsten could hear Dom tut before he dismissed the phone call. She laughed. They had discussed this only two months ago and he hadn't been happy, but as for Kirsten, it was one thing that she was looking forward to coming to the island. Trying to find Anna's missing sister would not be so amusing.

Chapter 9

Kirsten drove off the ferry into Lochmaddy and thought it the quaintest place she'd ever seen. It was like there was a loch almost beside every house or small housing estate. Plenty of water everywhere and she understood how Uist at times seemed to simply be barely above water at all. She found the play park that Dom had spoken about on her mobile phone, reading it off the maps function. She realised why he picked it, for there was a loop around it, a circular road system and several ways out. It wasn't ideal, not like when you're in the big city and there were multiple escape routes but at least there were a few, even if they all headed generally to the same place at the end.

If Dom was in the big city, he'd be able to hide amongst the number of people, but here he was making across moorland and would have done most of it while it was still dark. She wondered if the car had even been found, if anybody had noticed it burning. How far away from the houses had he been?

Here in the island your neighbours could be half a mile to a mile down the road, possibly even further depending on where you were. If he picked the right spot to burn the car it may even have gone unnoticed. Kirsten hoped so, praying that Dom had taken out a multiple-day hire so the car wouldn't be missed for a while at least.

When she first started the job, she used to worry about those people sitting waiting for their cars to be returned, but now they were just a casualty of their job, as long as they weren't actual casualties inside the vehicles. A car is just a car, but she backed Dom's decision to try and rescue the young man as well, although he was really nothing to them. He was a member of the public, one of those people that Kirsten's team protected even though they didn't know it.

Kirsten saw the play park was sitting off the road unnoticed and lurking beside it were a number of old boats, mere shells now. Some of the houses looked as if they were shells as well. The whole quaint feeling took a slightly different edge as she saw a building that was almost falling down. They never seemed to tidy up here, make everything good. Some things just got left to rot even if they were beside new builds. It was a bizarre feature of the islands, one that Kirsten had noted over and over again, but in other ways, it did give the place character. One of the more fastidious wouldn't have enjoyed it.

As Kirsten slowed down to stop beside one of the houses, she saw a man in the rear-view mirror jump out from a long strand of green angelica, white flowers at the top. It was obviously left from last year, for it had decayed somewhat, but was giving enough cover for him. Maybe he had been inside one of the old boats. Either way, Kirsten didn't care, she simply pushed open the door as Dom approached the car. He slipped inside and she drove off.

'Am I glad to see you,' said Dom. 'I'm starving; have you got any food?'

'Yes, let's make away somewhere. Down some track out of the way. We can stop, have a brief, and a think about how we're doing this.'

'There's plenty of roads coming away to nowhere,' said Dom.

Within five minutes, they pulled off through a side road. They couldn't see anyone about so Kirsten pulled out some of the sandwiches she had in the rear of the car, allowing Dom to eat. He surely must have been hungry. She had purchased a flask at one of the petrol stations along the route and filled it up with coffee that morning. Dom drank it heartily before taking in some more water as well from the plastic bottles Kirsten had in the boot of the car. As he finished munching and drinking, Kirsten pulled another box out from the boot. It was shallow and as she opened it, Dom shook his head.

'You've got to be kidding. You know what I look like when I put that stuff on.'

'Your face has been seen by the car-hire people. If that car has disappeared, we need to make sure you don't get spotted. Go on, there's a mirror in there as well.'

Kirsten stayed to one side watching Dom take on Grandpa protocol. She was amazed how in fifteen minutes' time the man now had a beard, a wig of grey hair and had changed into clothes that said, 'I'm at least seventy-five.' Of course, Dom was sprightlier than that but he even started to put on a walk and a slight limp.

'You'll be my daughter then,' said Dom.

'Granddaughter,' said Kirsten. 'I don't look like I'm middle-aged.'

'Oh, feisty. Anyway, come on. You better drive. You don't want an old man driving around. Do you think they've left the island?'

'I don't think so,' said Kirsten. 'It makes more sense if they're going to keep her, and keep her I think they should. After all, it's Anna's sister. Whoever it is that's taken her, if they want to find Anna, they might need to bring Anna to them in the end. Orla would be bait.'

'Or Linda,' said Dom. 'Whatever they call her.'

'Anna won't have told her where she is. She's not stupid enough to do that. She would never have taken Orla to any of the safe houses, but if they've got her, they might just be able to pull Anna out of the woodwork. We need to get her back and my bet is she's on one of these three islands. Failing that, we'll check Barra to the south. It's only a ferry ride away. Although moving her across a ferry would be difficult. They'd have to stick her in the back, which is why I think Barra would be good. It's not a long trip.'

'Now there's the trip north up to Harris and then Lewis. They could hide there,' said Dom.

'Yes, but that's more populated. Certainly, Lewis is, possibly Harris, but we'll start here, work our way through North Uist and then down, looking out for anything unusual.'

'I did see the van last night. I clocked the number plate, although it was dark, so I might have got the numbers wrong.'

'How badly off was the guy you took to the hospital?'

'Complete mess. They smashed him in the face several times with a gun butt. I mean he'll recover but his nose probably won't set right. I was worried about him, though. He was bleeding from the head and needed proper medical attention. I don't think a helicopter came in last night so they must have felt they were able to treat him.'

'You did the right thing, Dom,' said Kirsten. 'Now let's get going.'

Kirsten took the car first to the top of North Uist, then drove around going back through Lochmaddy then round the loop to the west side. She even ran right up to the north up to Rushgarry, Berneray, and Borve, watching where the ferry came in. Having gone around the loop several times, they stopped down at Clachan and were able to observe one of the main junctions in the island.

As they sat there, Kirsten watched the cars going past. Given the time of year, there weren't many tourists and Kirsten tried to pick out locals as they drove past. A large grey van approached, coming down from the north. Kirsten saw Dom staring at it intently.

'That's the same make. I thought last night it might have been a black van, but I wasn't that close. That's dark grey. No windows in the back. Follow that,' said Dom.

Kirsten needed no further invitation and pulled out some distance behind the van. She drove up beside it, overtaking it as if she was impatient, allowing Dom to get a good look at it. It continued south for a short distance before stopping, so Kirsten tried to ease down her speed. Looking behind her in the rear-view mirror, she saw someone get into the van and begin to turn around.

She turned her own car around, racing back up, but trying to keep it at a distance as she saw the van travelling northward again before taking a right out towards the Lochmaddy road. She didn't follow it on the road, instead stopping, letting it get a long distance ahead before she turned in to follow. As she did, she saw it take a right on a road she hadn't been on before. The junction was neat, and the sign said Locheport.

As soon as she took a right, Kirsten saw a house on the right hand side and more loch and water either side of the road that became a single track. She looked down at her phone, handing it to Dom.

'Find something on that that says why we're here.'

'There's some sculpture down the bottom. We're heading for it.'

The van was in the distance and the road incredibly straight. It was a single track and she had to stop at one point to allow someone coming the other way to pass. They continued to drive along, making their way past flat moorland with electricity lines running alongside the road. Kirsten began to feel she was really out into the unknown here, with only the occasional loch at the side to give her company. She saw the occasional sheep kicking about as well, but in general, everywhere seemed so barren.

As they approached a barn on the right-hand side, they saw that the van had pulled over, but Kirsten drove straight past. Once she got around the bend, the road now descended into a gravel track, no more a proper asphalt road. Kirsten continued to drive, pulling in behind a large stone house, making sure the car was out of sight from the road.

Together with Dom, she crossed the road into the field, and using a small pair of binoculars, stared at the house the van had stopped at. She saw a couple of men get out but there wasn't much untoward about them.

'We've got to be careful,' said Kirsten. 'It's going to be hard to approach here without being seen. They've picked a really good place. Quiet, off the track, but obvious. The only thing they haven't managed is to get two routes out.'

'I guess they took the option of the quiet. I mean, how many people will come down here? I know I said, there's that sculpture, but we're not in tourist season. You drive down here, you get to the end, you drive back. And the road's single track. There's a couple of houses about, some people here and there, but to be honest, I don't think anyone'll be here for that long. No one, except those who live here, and they're far enough away from them. '

'You're right, Dom.'

'I think it's best that we sit and watch. If they'd wanted her dead, they'd have killed her by now,' said Dom.

'Either way, making a forced attack now isn't going to get us anywhere. We've got to get up closer. We're going to have to wait till nightfall at least.'

'Good idea,' said Kirsten. 'We'll sit and wait it out. There's enough food in the car for us anyway. They shouldn't be able to see it on the other side of that building. To be honest, the building looks so run down I don't think anybody will be around here.'

'Best not to sit in the car though,' said Dom. 'Let's take the stuff out into the building. One of us can stay out here and watch while the other chills out. We might be able to find out what's going on with Carrie Anne and Justin.'

'I'm on first watch then,' said Kirsten.

'But you were up driving through the night,' said Dom. 'I'll take it, boss.'

'No, you won't. You've been out in the cold. Get in there and get some sleep. I can watch the building from here as well. That's an order.'

Dom nodded. Kirsten thought he looked like an old man when he walked across the road, back to the building. She lay down in the grass, feeling the snow-covered moss beneath it. As she stared at the building in front of her, she knew they'd have to bring things to a head sooner or later. Looking at her watch, she counted the hours until nightfall. Maybe she'd hear from Carrie Anne soon and then they'd know which way this whole deal was going.

Chapter 10

Carrie Anne sat in the lay-by surrounded by tall trees. She had picked up a hire car and would leave it in the lay-by when Justin turned up in one of the service vehicles. There were false number plates and fewer connections tied to the service car than there would be to the hire car and so it was wise to wait for Justin. She also needed backup going inside the building. With recent events, she was worried that they may not be the only people heading to Killen.

Killen was north of Glasgow, set out beyond some single carriageway roads, certainly not like the large motorways between Edinburgh and Glasgow. It felt like you were in the highlands, although those in the far north would complain they hadn't started yet. Carrie Anne was never bothered by such demarcations but instead stared at the snow around her, falling now on this higher ground.

The name kept ringing through her head. Walter. What did it mean, Walter? Justin had searched the databases and not found a Walter either, although he did say that he'd been reminded of Anna talking to her sister about a Walter. He'd thought that he was a man connected with the pair of them, but Carrie Anne was finding it hard to see how that meant anything, certainly not to do with the current issue.

They still had no idea what Anna had done other than she was being called a traitor. *But if she was, the analyst thought, why have we got all these sides coming and attacking us? If they know we're on a kill order, they'd keep out of the way, unless maybe they were the Russians coming for her. Maybe they were something entirely different.*

Carrie Anne hated her hair tied up. *God meant woman to have a proper mane of hair,* she thought. She was a woman who couldn't abide short hair and thought it worth the time to make sure that your hair looked good. Therefore, tying it up was a travesty. However, when in this work environment where she had to react quickly and often to disguise who she was, tying it up and tucking it away was the best option. It would need a wash tonight though, especially if she was any time under the balaclava.

She sat up as a car pulled in behind her and she saw Justin's smiling face in the rear-view mirror. He had made reasonable time from Inverness and as she stepped out of the car dressed in a leather jacket and dark jeans, she began to focus more intently on what they were about to do. She checked the inside of her coat making sure her weapon was there and then climbed in beside Justin, in the passenger seat of his car.

'Any word from the boss?'

'Right now, on the ferry. Seems to have made good progress anyway, and it was a fine drive down but thank you for asking,' said Justin.

'Okay, we drive up to the address, scout it out first,' said Carrie Anne.

'I have been in the field before,' said Justin.

'I'm not usually like this, but from when I read your record, you're more a man for meetings. First approaches, going and finding something you need as opposed to being under pressure, especially with others about.'

'Just relax,' said Justin. 'I can handle myself.'

'We nearly didn't in North Berwick. Armed and quick to kill they were. Head in the game, Justin. I mean that, for both our sakes.'

Carrie Anne was not often so serious, but North Berwick had scared her. She'd barely dropped to her knees when the man was dispatched right in front of her. It could have been her. Her senses were heightened now.

Justin pulled out of the lay-by and drove down through more wooded roads towards Killen. As he approached the village, he took a turn down to a lane that headed off up a small track where they saw a house at the end.

'Stop short,' said Carrie Anne. 'We'll walk it up from here. We don't want to go into the driveway like we own the place.'

'So, we're not just going up to the front door then?' said Justin.

'Hope you got your boots on you,' she said. 'We'll come in around the back. There's quite a lot of wood here. That'll be good cover, but also will be good cover for anybody else.'

She stepped out of the car and slowly walked over to where she saw a path disappearing off into the woods. She motioned at Justin to follow. Together they walked five hundred yards to a spot that lay behind the house.

The intention of the house was to be white, but it ended up a more of a drab cream from the weather beating it had taken over the years. There were two stories, possibly three bedrooms, three rooms downstairs.

Carrie Anne cut off through the wood approaching the back

garden, noticing that it was no smooth lawn but simply a hodgepodge of reclaimed land. Any mower would have to be able to conduct a hill start, looking at it. In fact, most of the grass seemed to be moss, that she could see had avoided the snow, but there were a number of animals running around through the branches of the trees. She swore she saw squirrels, possibly even red ones.

Carrie Anne motioned Justin to follow her. She raced across the lawn up to the windows of the house, looking in and seeing no one. She drew her weapon, approached the back door, and tried the handle. The handle turned. She pushed the door open gently, moving in low.

Pointing her gun all around, she scanned the inside kitchen. She motioned Justin through the door to the right reckoning it'd take them through to possibly a living room, while she headed through another that ended in a hallway. There were no coats hanging up and the house had a cold feel about it as if the heating hadn't been on in a while.

Carrie Anne climbed the stairs, stepping to the outside of them as soon as she heard the middle creak. Slowly, she scanned through three bedrooms, finding a pile of romantic comedy books. She struggled to work out how this could be Anna Hunt's place. There were pictures of people she didn't recognise but they were different in each room. She reckoned it was Anna's attempt to giving a family feel to the place.

Carrie Anne stole through, opening wardrobes and finding the bare minimum of clothes. She recognised that most could be operational, the sort of clothing that was hard-wearing, dark, blending you into the night, but there were also greens that could be used if you were out in the field, although at the moment, the white would show you up. She looked out of the bedroom window and saw that the snow was lying in certain places. The lawn had obviously been hit by the sun, for most of the snow there had melted. At the front, she saw patches of snow and ice, and again felt a shiver from the house.

There came a thud from downstairs. Carrie Anne held her weapon close and glided quickly to the stairs, looking down, but she could see no one. Slowly, she crept down, wondering whether she could call out for Justin or not. If she did, she would warn anyone else who was here that she was there, maybe make herself an open target. Inside, she cursed herself for letting Justin go off on his own, having bought that he was an experienced operator.

He was, but in very different situations. Prisoner handovers, bring Justin in. Going into a situation where they didn't know you were coming, bring Justin in, but this was different. Somebody was watching them. You had to be more careful, more observant. It wasn't Justin's forte. Carrie Anne slowly descended the stairs and crept along the hallway. Her heart was beating fast now, but she heard something in the living room. There was movement. It sounded like somebody was pouring a drink. *Justin wouldn't be so daft, would he? Is this what this was? He simply needed to refresh himself?* You didn't do that while you were on this sort of a mission.

Carrie Anne moved closer to the door, listening intently. There were some footsteps, not very distinct. She thought she heard breathing, and a drink was being drunk, but that was from a different place in the room. She swore there was more than one person in there.

Carrie Anne reached down for the handle of the door and gripped her weapon even tighter. If she was quick, she might be able to surprise him. With her left hand, she pushed the door wide open, stepped in with her gun raised high, and then saw Justin sitting on the chair, a gun at his head. There wasn't just one, there was two pointing at him, another from a man to the left of her.

They had removed Justin's balaclava, taking a good look at him. The three men were not wearing any face coverings themselves. A third man stood across the room, polishing off the whisky that had been poured.

'I hear you're after Anna Hunt,' said a man in a Russian accent. 'Why do you want her? Who are you?' he said.

'Easy,' said Carrie Anne. Her eyes sweeping the room constantly trying to keep all three men in check. Her gun was still raised, but the man who had spoken didn't seem concerned, and continued to drink the whisky in the tumbler. The other two men, however, focused their guns at Justin.

Justin was nervous; his legs shaking, he began to tap his foot on the ground. Carrie Anne could see the sweat coming from him. He must have assessed them; must have seen they were real. *This was not some amateur crew*, she thought.

Carrie Anne stepped further into the room, but slowly moving over towards the man with the whisky tumbler.

'I could ask you the same thing. Why are you looking for Anna Hunt? What does Russia want with Anna Hunt?'

'You're the analyst. You tell me,' said the man. The accent was thick. Carrie Anne was struggling to look at the man's face while keeping her eye on the other two. She was outgunned completely.

'I seem to have you at a disadvantage. Why don't you put your gun down? Then maybe we can talk.'

'No,' said Carrie Anne. 'I put my gun down, you'll put one to my head as well.'

'I like you. They said analyst, but I looked at your profile. I thought, "she is a woman who knows what she wants. She's a cat. Good to look at, but cunning. If she takes a swipe with her claws, you'll get hurt."'

Carrie Anne was ignoring the man, studying the other men, her eyes sweeping back and forward, formulating a plan. She was trying to calculate the odds of getting out of here alive with Justin, as opposed to without Justin. She didn't want to leave him, but if trying to secure his rescue would end up in her death as well, that would seem to be pretty pointless.

Sweat was forming underneath her balaclava. She could feel it run down past her nose, into the wells of her eyes, stinging them. *Come on*, she thought. *What do we do? Where do we go from here?'*

'So, my cat, what say you and I get cosy and have a chat? I wouldn't want to see a woman like you wasted. Maybe you could switch sides as well.'

Had she switched sides? thought Carrie Anne. *Had Anna really done it? It didn't seem like her. Wasn't her style. Something about this didn't seem right.*

'Put the gun down and we'll talk. You could all join her as a team, couldn't you? You could all come to her. My little cat,' said the man and he stepped forward putting a hand up to Carrie Anne's balaclava. 'Let's see that face,' he said. Carrie Anne allowed him to reach up and start to pull the balaclava off.

'Yes, fabulous,' he said. Then she saw it. The two men looking, the momentary distraction. The closest to Justin had tilted his weapon just slightly away, and the other wasn't pointing at Justin at all.

Carrie Anne fired two quick shots. The first caught the

man standing beside Justin clean in the temple, causing him to topple over. The second hit the man across the room square between the eyes. The man beside her grabbed her hair, and tried to throw a punch into her, but Carrie Anne blocked the punch, drove an elbow into his stomach, and pushed him back into the wall behind him. She saw him reach for a weapon, brought her own around and dispatched him with a clean shot to the head.

The sweat ran from her face, and she blinked her eyes, trying to keep it from running into them. She looked around for her hair tie that had fallen when the man had taken her balaclava off. She picked it up, pulled her hair together and tied it up again before putting the balaclava back over. She went over to Justin who was sitting in the chair breathing heavily.

'Are you okay?' she said.

'Yes,' he said, 'very definitely. I'm okay.' The silencer in the end of her gun had prevented the fight becoming something that would arouse the suspicion of any neighbours of the house, but Carrie Anne wasn't for waiting around. If there were three of them in the house, there may be more people outside. There may be people expecting a call.

She pulled Justin up to his feet. 'Search,' she said. 'I've done upstairs. Search.' She saw him jittery at first, but eventually start to go through bookcases, round the drinks' cabinet. The gloves they wore would leave no marks, but Carrie Anne was worried that with the balaclavas off, they may have left any DNA on their hair behind. Not that her DNA was on any database.

Justin bent down and was sweeping a hand underneath the couch when he pulled something out.

'What's that?' asked Carrie Anne, stepping over one of the

bodies of the men she had shot.

'It's a post-it note saying "Walter".'

'It's just like the one we found in North Berwick,' said Carrie Anne. 'We need to find Walter,' she said. 'Justin, that's our top priority. That'll find us Anna.'

'I've already told boss,' said Justin. 'The only Walter I can find associated is the Walter Anna said about her sister. They used to go to Walter.'

'Then we best hope the boss can get her sister. In the meantime, time to move out and check the area. I want to know who these guys were.'

Almost casually, Carrie Anne pulled out her mobile phone and photographed the three faces of the men that lay dead on the floor. Justin shook his head and made to go for the exit, but Carrie Anne told him to wait. The man was clearly shaken about what she'd done, as she was, trembling a little inside, but she reckoned they'd meant business. She believed that the pair of them wouldn't have been leaving if she put her gun down.

As they made their way back out through the wood and down to the car, Carrie Anne remembered what was on a report, something Anna Hunt had written about her. *Can be distracted by attention from male parties.*

Anna once told her that you never wrote a true appraisal of anyone because if you were too accurate and somebody got hold of it, they would have all the detail they needed. The one thing that never went from Carrie Anne was her focus. It seemed that Anna's ploy had worked. It may have been why Justin was still alive. *Good old Anna,* thought Carrie Anne.

Chapter 11

Kirsten received a call from Carrie Anne telling of their close escape. She now noted that her team had been put into three extremely dangerous situations, all with the potential to wipe out some of the members. What was bugging her was that while they were on a kill order for Anna Hunt, none of the threats had seemed to come from Anna but had come from elsewhere. She tried to take some time off late that afternoon, waiting for night to fall, and leaving Dom to watch the house where Linda was being kept. But she'd struggled to sleep, turning over and over her mind the idea that Anna could have defected, that she was in some way a traitor. It just didn't sit.

She wondered if she was being played, controlled. It was bothering Kirsten. When she'd been in the police force, it had always been Macleod who was leading the team, and then had come Hope McGrath. It was structured. You understood, if McGrath had got an instruction, it had come down from Macleod. If Macleod had got an instruction, you knew where that had come from. He didn't have somebody else just pitching in. It went all the way up to the Chief Constable, not that she'd ever had anything from him.

Here in the service, it was different. People took over missions. Yes, there were people up there, but you were never quite sure who was running what. The whole thing was so compartmentalised that you never got a full picture, never a full understanding, but then that was the point of this spy stuff, wasn't it? Everything was packaged up, so if anything fell through, only so many people would know. The trouble was that when you were trying to work out anything then from the bottom, you didn't know who knew what. Knowing who to trust was hard, and yet the system was set up to allow so little trust. Trusting was the most difficult thing to do, because you never really got to know people on a wider basis.

But Kirsten trusted her team, and when she went out to meet Dom watching the house, she didn't question his motives on that previous night, didn't question his intentions of not moving in during daylight to pick up Linda. It now looked like a mistake. But he was trying to keep things quiet, to be discreet. That was the job as a spy, to be discreet, and yet these people were not discreet at all. Russians. At least Russian accents being bandied about.

Worse still, her mind kept replaying the problem that Craig was seen in North Berwick. You couldn't bring emotion into this game. That's what they told you, but they should let you talk to people outside about it. She could sit and chew it over with Macleod, her former boss in the police force because he'd have things to say. He wouldn't approve of a lot of stuff, but he'd be a good sounding board.

But she wasn't allowed that, so instead, she had found Craig, a driver from London. The guy seemed to be much more than a driver. Someone she shared confidences with, close personal things, but not any of this spy business, because he was in it as well. She'd never been able to give him any detail, and yet here he was, in the midst of all of this.

Kirsten needed answers fast because it was all playing on her mind. As Kirsten approached Dom in the darkness, he sat buried in the field. There were blobs of white all around, for it had snowed that afternoon. Although it wasn't thick, it was enough to make her feel the cold through her legs as she knelt down on it.

'Any movement?' Kirsten whispered.

'All still in there. Light's still on. I've heard nothing significant.'

'Then I'm going to approach,' said Kirsten.

'You think that's wise?' asked Dom.

'We need to get the lay of the land. I'm the best to do this, you know that. And I want you to sit here on point. Feed me in via the earpiece if anything's up, if you see anybody else arrive. I'm not going in to extract, I'm just going to get a sounding board for what we're up against. Then when I come back, we'll talk about pulling Linda out of there. Given what's gone on earlier, I expect extreme prejudice if we interfere, and I don't really want a fire fight with such a number of them and the two of us.'

Dom nodded and watched as Kirsten stalked across the grass. Although she walked forward, she was crouching low. She clambered through a ditch and up closer to the house. There was a gravel path around it and Kirsten did her best not to make a sound as she crossed it. Being light on your feet was important, always.

She could hear a few laughs as she approached. Slowly, she crept up alongside of the house and then stopped dead as she heard a door opening. In front of her, a light came on and a man stepped out, lighting up a cigarette, and began to smoke. He looked left and right, but he couldn't see Kirsten twenty feet away in the darkness.

She slowed her breathing down, one hand on the weapon beside her, watching in case he would spot her. She was also taking care to check that he might pretend he hadn't seen her before walking back inside, but their eyes never met. She crouched there for three minutes. The man drew the smoke in from the cigarette before eventually chucking the butt away onto the driveway. He closed the door behind him, and thirty seconds later the light went out.

Kirsten breathed a sigh of relief, but didn't hang about, stalking up to the house. She went up to a window and listened in but could hear nothing. Cautiously, she put her little mirror up, using it to look inside, but the room was dark. Bringing the mirror back down, she moved on round to the front of the house, realising she was becoming exposed, for the track that led up to it was now in front of her.

'Watch the road closely,' she whispered on her comms link to Dom. 'I'm out in the open now. If any car comes in, it'll light me up.'

'Roger,' said Dom.

Kirsten took her mirror out again and put it up to see into the window above her. She could tell that there were lights inside, but they weren't the normal ones, or at least they were being heavily dampened by the curtain. She could see it was a curtain, and she had to stand up, lifting the mirror much higher till she could find a gap where the drapes were brought together. She tried to remain calm as she saw the scene before her.

There were three men sitting on chairs, drinking beer and

smoking. At the centre of their half-circle was a woman stripped to her underwear and whose face looked as if it had been beaten. Kirsten could see other marks on her and wondered what ordeal she'd been put through.

'Dom, we're getting her out in the next hour,' said Kirsten. 'They're trying to force information from her.'

Kirsten looked closely in the little mirror and watched as one of the men stepped forward, pressing a cigarette butt into the woman's arm. She wondered why she didn't squeal, but then Kirsten saw the gag across her mouth. Once the man had finished pushing the butt in, he threw it away. He told her to tell him where Anna was. The woman shook her head and the gag was removed.

'I don't bloody know,' the woman screamed at him. 'She's not stupid enough to tell me. You can all just—'

Whatever curse or swear the woman was bringing to them, it was dispatched with the back of a hand by one of the men. Kirsten could see the woman in tears, the eyes streaming, and as she went to shout again the gag was reintroduced. One of the men turned towards the window and Kirsten dropped down with the mirror. From the light in front of her which suddenly increased, she realised the curtains had been opened. Not fully, because there was a small tight beam of light that came out, shining on the thin layer of snow that lay about.

Carefully, Kirsten moved to one side.

'Seen four, Dom,' Kirsten whispered, checking the other side of the building. She stole quickly round in front of another window and looked into a dark room. A fourth window had curtains across it. As she put her mirror up to see in, she thought she caught at least another two figures.

'A minimum of six, Dom,' she said. 'This is going to be

difficult to do, but we need to get in quick. I'm coming back to your position.'

'Roger,' was the only reply from Dom.

As she traversed back across, Kirsten could feel the anger rising within her. She'd grown used to the idea that people would be tortured in this business, but after some of her recent events, she'd realised how brutal people could be. Yet it hadn't prepared her for seeing a woman being tortured. She hadn't seen the worst of it, no doubt. Who knows what they would do to her? A woman on her own.

The thing was that Linda was probably correct. Anna would be not stupid enough to give her any information, and in fact, if she had, Kirsten would be suspicious of it, treating it as a possible decoy. It was only the idea of Walter that made Kirsten know she had to get Linda out for professional reasons. To get her away from the hands of these men, that was a personal reason, one that any decent human being would try to do. Kirsten wanted to make sure that the decency that she'd had back in the police force didn't leave her now that she was in the spy game, but there were hard decisions to be made at times. However, this was not one of them.

She sidled up to Dom. He looked at her face, although it was dark. She was sure he could make out the concern.

'Did it look like she was holding up? Do you think we're too late?' he asked.

'Don't beat yourself up. It's not your fault. You played it right. Well, you played a good line, just didn't work out this time.' Kirsten saw Dom's worried face. 'But you'll get your chance,' she said. 'We're going to go out and get her. With at least six, though, we're going to have to be quick. It's going to be run in, take them down room by room, quick. Soon as we see her, grab and go.'

'And where to?' asked Dom. 'Where do we take her from here?'

'Out in the car, stay low. We take the ferry tomorrow up to Harris. I've got contacts up there. Once we get up into Lewis we'll head for one of the safe houses on the mainland via the ferry, or I might see if I can hire a boat over.'

'You don't want to bring anybody into this you don't have to,' said Dom. 'Too risky.'

'I'm well aware of that, Dom,' said Kirsten, 'but we need to get that woman out. Extreme prejudice, shoot to kill. I don't think they'll hesitate to kill us.'

'Did they have accents?' Dom asked. 'Could you hear them talk?'

'Not very well. Carrie Anne said they were Russian in Killen. I thought they were fake Russian, in Berwick. I still think something's being played here, Dom. I really do.'

Kirsten returned to the car and came back with some other ammunition for Dom. Together they had a couple of handguns, all with silencers, but she'd also packed a couple of smoke grenades if needed.

'In from the rear,' said Kirsten, 'and in through that door is the closest to where she is. If need be, we can defend her from in there, go out through the window if we have to.'

'Understood,' said Dom. Kirsten watched him take a moment. He seemed to go on his knee and whisper something.

'I didn't realise you were religious,' said Kirsten.

'I haven't got my guardian angel with me,' he said. Kirsten gave him a confused look.

'Carrie Anne. Ask Justin.'

'You've got me,' said Kirsten.

'No offense,' said Dom, 'but Carrie Anne seems to look after us old men.'

Kirsten shook her head and told him to get ready.

Slowly they crept forward across the darkness of the night until they came close to the house. At that point, someone stepped out and they both went to the ground. A man started up the van. The door was opened and suddenly they saw Linda, clothed now, dragged out to the van. The door was shut, the lights of the van came on and it began driving away.

'Bollocks,' said Kirsten, and looked at Dom. 'Back to the car, quick.'

Chapter 12

Kirsten didn't switch on the car headlights as they followed the van ahead of them. She had to remain at a reasonable distance, given the fact that they were on a very straight road, remote, and she didn't want the man ahead in the van to know that they were behind them. On reaching the end of the road, the man turned left, taking them to the main junction in North Uist. If they'd taken a left, they would've driven down towards Benbecula. Instead, they took a right, heading on the west circular route around North Uist. Kirsten kept well back at the junction because of the streetlights that were in effect, but as soon as the van was clear, she followed, determined not to lose her prey ahead.

'Wherever they're taking her at this time at night, it's not going to be good,' said Dom.

'You think this could be it?' asked Kirsten. 'They're actually going to get rid of her?'

'Well, it makes sense if she hasn't got anything to say because she knows nothing, and they believe that. The last thing they need is her being left alive. As far as they're aware, her boyfriend might be dead. I reckon they'll set something up.'

The car continued in silence with both occupants worried

about Linda's fate. A few miles up the road, the van took a left. Kirsten followed, watching it disappear over towards the cliffs on the west side of Uist. Kirsten turned her own car into a field, parking it behind a hedge before she and Dom snuck up towards where the van had gone. She could see a field at the end of the track and there was a car sitting there. Dom picked out his binoculars and peering through them, he reported back to Kirsten.

'I think I can see her. There's certainly somebody inside that car, but they look motionless.'

'What's the point of putting her in a car?' asked Kirsten.

'Well, it isn't coming back down the track,' said Dom. 'That field is quite steep there. I reckon they're going to push it.'

'Push it?' Kirsten looked over to see the field heading down towards the cliffs. There was a hedge running across with a gap in the middle, but outside of that, there was nothing to stop the car, if it had enough speed, to go through the grass and get over the cliff.

'They're going to make it look like a botched burglary or something.'

'You could be right, Dom. Stay up here. I'm going to go down this field and get parallel with them.'

'And do what?' said Dom.

'If they push that car down, I might have a chance to get in and get her out.'

'What? That's not going to happen,' said Dom. 'You're not going to have time.'

'Just watch me.' Kirsten tore off down the field.

Dom put the binoculars back up to his eyes, Linda's captors now lighting some sort of a brand. The yellow glow lit up the night, the brightest thing around. Dom watched the men try and crowd round it to shield it and he wondered what they were doing at the rear of the car. Then it occurred to him that they were at the petrol cap. It was being opened and maybe the brand was going to be put inside.

There seemed to be a lot of commotion amongst the men. Then someone opened the front door of the car, did something inside, and then got back out, closing the door. Dom turned the binoculars back to the rear of the car. He saw the brand being inserted into the engine. The flame was at the end of the brand, but it was working its way down, and Dom realised what they were going to do.

Sure enough, the car was let go. As it started to trundle down the field, Dom could see the yellow glow disappear out towards the sea. He tapped his comms link.

'Kirsten, they've got a flaming brand in the petrol tank. You won't have time.'

'I can see it,' said Kirsten. 'If she's awake, we might just be able to do it as long as they haven't tied her in.'

'And if they have?' said Dom, but there was no answer. As he turned the binoculars toward the field below him, he saw a black shadow running along, her head barely above the hedge at the end of the field. He turned the binoculars back towards the men who seemed to be laughing and turning away from the accident that was about to happen. When he turned the binoculars back, he could barely see Kirsten arriving at the car.

Kirsten watched the orange glow as it came down the field, and as the car broke through the hedge, she ran to meet it. There wasn't that much more field left. Soon it would be over the hedge.

She ran over, grabbing hold of the car door. As she pulled

it open, her top hand grabbed the roof rail and she swung her legs in as soon as the space between the door and the car allowed. Kirsten threw herself inside, was jolted, and felt the car hit her on the side. There was a pain up at her ribs, but she ignored it as she moved her knees round, positioning herself in the passenger seat and was almost nutted by Linda jiggling about.

The woman seemed to be out cold, but she was belted in and Kirsten reached down, clicking the red button straightaway and throwing the belt off. She reached over, pushing open the car door, and desperately put her hand underneath Linda's backside. She pushed the woman with all her might, but the legs slid up, dropping behind the steering wheel, while the rest of her body was hanging out of the car.

Kirsten looked left and could see the cliff approaching. She'd only have about five more seconds. She pushed down hard on the woman's legs, forcing them down and wondering if she heard a crack. Regardless, they slipped out from under the seat. Linda tipped more violently, her legs now up towards the ceiling. Kirsten pushed down on her seat with her own legs driving forward out through the door, driving a shoulder up into Linda's buttocks. They fell out like two sacks of potatoes, Linda coming out head first and flopping over while Kirsten reached out, desperately trying to grab ground.

The momentum of the car was making them slide down the cliff. Behind them, the flaming brand was so close to the petrol tank that it lit up the cliff edge, allowing Kirsten to see and reach out with one hand. She grabbed it desperately, swinging her legs around into the cliff. As she pulled herself up with that one hand, she threw up a second hand but was then hit by Linda's rolling body, still with enough momentum to keep her moving.

Kirsten's arm screamed. As Linda hit her, the woman's legs dropped over the side. Kirsten released one hand, throwing her arm around Linda's waist. The woman was clearly still out cold despite the crack that had happened to her legs in the car. Kirsten clung on desperately. Beneath her there came an explosion. She felt the heat rise, but worse than that was the force from the explosion making her rock . . . and her hand began to slip.

She wondered if the men would come to have a look to see what had happened, but she couldn't think about that as she felt her shoulders about to separate, hanging on with one hand and holding Linda around the waist with the other arm. She wanted to scream for Dom, but that would bring attention. Surely, he'd have the wit to come down. Dear God, please.

Linda's eyes suddenly flicked open, and she stared first at Kirsten's face, then she looked down below her and could hear the crashing waves.

'Don't scream,' said Kirsten, running out of breath. 'You scream, we die. Hold on.' Kirsten tried to dig her feet into the cliff edge but every time she pushed, a small piece of rock would fall away.

'Where are the men?' said Linda suddenly. 'Where are they? How am I here? . . . ?'

'Just hold onto me,' said Kirsten. 'Hold onto me and I'll get you out of this.'

Linda's face didn't seem to believe Kirsten and the woman's eyes were wide with terror, but she didn't scream. Whether that was because she was too afraid because of her current situation or whether it was because of the men that might come, Kirsten would never know. But Kirsten could feel her hand begin to slip.

'I'm going to push you up. You need to reach with both hands and get yourself over the edge,' said Kirsten. 'Do you understand me? I haven't got time to explain further.'

There was a nod and Kirsten pulled down with her left arm, pushing up with her right, driving Linda up as far as she could. The woman didn't seem to be taking any weight and Kirsten's left arm began to slide.

'Get up there. I'm going,' said Kirsten as loud as she dared. This seemed to jolt Linda into moving but that increased the weight down on Kirsten's arm. Her left hand slipped once and then she felt it come loose.

Terror tore through Kirsten with the sudden realisation she was going to fall, that she was not going to be around anymore. For a split second, everything stood still. Everything seemed to fade into dark.

And then a hand grabbed hers. She continued to descend another foot and then Dom's face was over the edge, two arms now down, pulling her up.

'No further. Calm, easy,' said Dom, and he pulled as hard as he could. Kirsten flung her right arm up reaching high and grabbing his elbow and then dragged herself up either side of his arms.

'Lie on me,' she heard Dom exclaim and realised he wanted Linda to sit on top of him. Kirsten's shoulder blades felt like they were about to rip out of her back, but she dragged herself up onto Dom's shoulders, pulled herself before he turned, throwing her legs back over the cliff edge. All three lay there breathing heavily.

'Where are the men?' whispered Kirsten.

'Gone,' said Dom. 'Took the truck.'

There was a cry of pain from beside them. 'Sorry,' said Linda. 'This is broke. This is . . . '

'Going to have to wait,' said Kirsten. 'What have you got on you, Dom? We'll have to carry her.'

Dom took off his jacket, putting it around Linda and then undid the belt of his trousers. He strapped her ankles together as best he could, but the woman was clearly still in pain.

'We'll have to carry her to the car,' said Dom. 'I'll take shoulders, you take the rear. Try and keep her legs as straight as possible.'

Kirsten nodded, breathing heavily. It had taken a lot out of her, and her shoulders were as painful as she could remember them, but she picked up Linda by the legs, trying to hold them just in front of where she suspected the break was.

They trudged across the field beyond the hedge and made their way back up towards the car. The going was slow, not simply because it was dark but because Kirsten was so fatigued. Dom reminded her several times that she was dropping her patient, not carrying her as level as he wanted. She could hear the odd wince in pain and knew Linda was doing her best.

When they reached the car, they put her into the rear, laying her down. As the car light came on, Kirsten could see the full extent of the damage on Linda's face. The men had been brutal with her and a part of her wanted to go after them, to punish them. But the key thing was at least she was alive. If they went back after the men, they could lead her back into that same trouble. Linda was alive, able to talk, but she needed medical help.

Kirsten got into the driver's seat and looked at Dom beside her. 'You still want to make for the ferry?' he said.

'Absolutely,' said Kirsten. 'There's people up there I can

leave this woman with. I know people in the Stornoway police. She's of no use to anybody. They're not going to come after her again. For all I know she told them everything, so what's she going to tell the police? Once we get her in there, it'll be too risky for them to come and get her. Better for them to clear out.'

'But somebody will need to take her long term,' said Dom. 'Who can we trust? The police force will ask questions. Unless somebody comes in and hushes them up.'

'We need to get word back to Control then,' said Kirsten. 'That'd be the correct thing to do.'

'Are you sure about that?'

'I need someone on our side I can trust.' Kirsten's mind wheeled away. The new Control she didn't know. The rest of the people involved were her team and Anna. She'd have to bring somebody inside. Somebody who knew what she was talking about at some degree. Maybe she'd call London. Godfrey. How on earth would she contact Godfrey? He was the man she'd met that first time. He would be able to help. Anna had seemed to trust him. So, if he thought that Anna had turned, then maybe it would be true. But she'd need a way to contact him.

The car fell into silence as they drove through the night, eager to make the ferry the following morning. It would be a short hour's trip over to Harris and from there about an hour and a half up to Stornoway. She could deposit Linda with the police there and get her to hospital. As she drove along, Kirsten felt on edge. Who could she trust? How did she get a message to Godfrey? There looked like there was no easy answer.

Chapter 13

Kirsten slammed down the phone, sore, and marched over to the other side of the room. She poured herself a large black coffee, took an enormous gulp and found it burning her mouth, and had to fight not to spit it out there and then. Across from her in the room lying on a makeshift bed was Linda and a doctor from the Western Isles Hospital. He had rigged up a drip and was checking her over.

In the meantime, Kirsten had been trying to contact London on the phone, but everything she did seemed to end up in her call being denied. There was no clearance she could give to speak to anyone except those who answered the phone. As she thumped her hand on the desk again, the door opened and Detective Sergeant Andrea Lumley walked in.

Kirsten had met her before when she had protected a child on the Isle of Lewis. Although at times, she found Lumley difficult to deal with, the woman was sound and had helped her before. With stylishly groomed blonde hair descending to her shoulders, Andrea Lumley gave off the air of someone professional going about her job and who took no nonsense.

'A word if you don't mind,' said Andrea.

'Of course,' said Kirsten, making her way over to the corner of the room.

'I don't want to say anything in front of the victim over there,' said Andrea, 'but what am I meant to do with this? You come in, and the woman's almost beaten to death. Personally, I'd be asking if she had more than that done to her. Doctor says she's got cigarette burns on the side of her arms. Is she some sort of suspect? Are you probing her for information?'

'We weren't,' said Kirsten. 'Someone else was. Look, I know this is strange, but at the moment with what's going on, I need someone I can trust. All I want you to do is to keep her safe. Get her to the hospital if the doctor says she has to go. Get her attention, but make sure she stays safe.'

'And what? Just let you walk out? I don't get to be that simple in my reports. I have to put down what happened.'

'Then do that. Put down that a member of the services turned up with a woman that needed medical attention and protection. The operative would not give the reason for the protection. I'm fine with that,' said Kirsten.

Lumley stared at her, peering over her nose.

'You know what,' she said, 'I will look after that woman. It'd be nice though if it wasn't you coming in here. I want a nice man. Somebody that could charm me to do these things, instead of it just feeling like a chore.'

'Or just the right thing to do,' said Kirsten. She gave a bit of a smile though, as she trapped the detective, but Dom interrupted them.

'Sorry, excuse me. Boss, did you say you wanted to talk to Linda before we had to get out of here?'

'See, you should have come in with him,' said Andrea. 'He could have come along, told me things, I'd have accepted it quite happily.' Kirsten looked up at Dom and realised that the two of them were about the same age.

'He's too smooth. I wouldn't do that to you. I wanted you to do it of your own volition.'

'Look, I'm going to have to start relating this to people soon. Okay, the doctor is going to walk out of here. You're not going to have a lot of time. Go and talk to her, then get out of here.'

'Thank you,' said Kirsten. 'I still don't know where I'm going to go.' With that, she stood up and joined Dom. Walking across the room, she briefly asked the doctor if it was okay to speak to Linda, and he gave a nod. She seemed a little woozy, not quite with it, but Dom snapped his fingers in front of her face, bringing her back to attention.

'Linda, look, we need to know. You said that Anna never told you where she would meet, where she could hide out. You must have had places. Did she ever speak to you about safe houses?'

'No. The key thing about her life was that I didn't know anything about it.'

'But how would she get in touch with you then if she was in trouble or she needed you to . . .?'

'If she was in trouble, there's no way she'd have me near her. The last thing she wanted to do was put me in any position. You need to understand that.'

Kirsten raised her eyes to the ceiling, blew out a long breath. 'Who's Walter?' she asked.

'Walter?' said Linda. 'I've never known a Walter.'

'Has Anna ever known a Walter?' asked Dom.

'Not that I'm aware of. Certainly doesn't come from her private life. Why? Why did you want to know about Walter?'

'She left two posts-it notes in safe houses she has. They said "Walter". Is there anything about Walter? Think back. Walter.'

Linda sat back and closed her eyes. After a moment, Kirsten could see her give a brief smile. 'Waltzer,' she said. 'It's the Waltzer.'

'What?' said Kirsten. 'What do you mean?'

'Anna and I grew up not far from Aberdeen, and we'd go along to the amusement park there. She's younger than me. When she was really small, she always said she wanted to go on the Waltzer, but she couldn't pronounce it. 'Take me on the Walter, take me on the Walter. I love the Walter."

'So, the Waltzer is Walter,' said Kirsten.

Dom whispered in her ear, 'Do you really think so?'

'She wrote it twice,' said Kirsten, and turning back to Linda she asked, 'Where is that amusement park in Aberdeen?'

'Down near the coast. It's the famous one. You can't miss it. Everybody in Aberdeen knows it. Why? Do you think she could be there?'

'Linda,' said Kirsten, 'listen to me very carefully. I never asked you that question. Anybody else asks, you have no idea. You don't where it is, you don't know who Walter is. Okay? You've never heard of a Walter and I never asked you about him.'

'Okay,' said Linda,' I understand you.' As Kirsten went to turn away, Linda reached out with her hand, grabbing Kirsten's forearm. 'Look, just get her safe, okay?' Kirsten smiled. She definitely did not want to pass on the fact that Kirsten had been sent out to kill Anna, to take her down for treason.

'She's a good one,' said Linda, 'the best. Anna would do anything for this country. She already has, so you just find her and keep her safe. Listen, I just wanted to say thank you for coming for me.'

'I'm sorry I couldn't get here earlier,' said Kirsten. 'I hope you can recover from this.'

'Doc says the break's not too bad, although it feels bad enough. If you hadn't done that, I'd have been dead.'

'I'd have been dead with you,' said Kirsten. 'You just rest up and get better. Detective Lumley over there, she's going to look after you. She's a good one. Don't go anywhere until she says it's okay. I'll contact if there's further issues.'

The woman nodded. Kirsten made her way back across the room.

'That of any use?' asked Lumley.

'Very much, but don't ask why. Can I just ask one more thing of you?'

'What?' asked Lumley rather abruptly.

'I'll give you a ring when it's safe for her to move about again. Until then, don't let her out of police sight. Don't let her out of *your* sight.'

'What are you suggesting? She comes out of hospital and stays with me?'

Kirsten put on her most serious of faces. 'Yes. Simple.'

Lumley shook her head. 'What is it with you guys? You just swan in with all your problems and dump them on other people. Do you know the crap I got from the last time?'

'You saved a child's life doing it last time. You might save hers too.'

Dom and Kirsten made their way out to the car in the station rear car park where they sat staring at the wall opposite.

'So, we know it's Walter, the Waltzer in Aberdeen,' said Dom. 'So what, who do we tell? You're still going to need somebody to come in and help Lumley. Lumley can't take this forever. I know you told her to keep her in the house, but that's not going to happen, is it?'

'No. We need a word through to Godfrey as well. I think we're going to have to try and risk something.'

'What?' asked Dom.

'I think I know somebody who might be trustworthy. If he's not, we'll soon find out.'

'Do you know him to be?'

'Well, he's never let me down.'

'Who?' asked Dom. Kirsten didn't want to mention whom she'd been with and why, she just simply said the driver down in London, the one that took them to Control. 'How do you know he's clean? Did you know him from before?' Kirsten nodded. 'Carrie Anne said he was at the house in North Berwick.'

'I think there's different angles being played,' said Kirsten. 'I want to know what some of them are. Let's bring him along. Bring him in, see what happens. Because if we don't, I'm going to be doubting myself about him.'

'Okay,' said Dom, 'but just for the record, I think it's a risky manoeuvre. I'm not that keen on it.'

'You're not that keen on anything, but I hear you, Dom. I do hear you.' Kirsten sat in the car and picked up her phone. She dialled a number and then got a voice on the other end. 'I didn't think you'd call. Off the grid is what I heard.'

'What have you heard?' asked Kirsten.

'I know a little bit. They're saying Anna Hunt's gone bad. Is it true?'

'Don't know yet,' said Kirsten, trying to keep her options open with the man. 'All I know is that we're going to have to find out.'

'Did you call for a social chat or is it work?'

'It's work. Have you heard anything about Anna Hunt other

than that?'

'I've not been involved,' he said. 'I try to stay well clear of those things.'

'Well, I need to meet. I'm going to Aberdeen. It'll take me a day to get there. I need you to get a message to Godfrey.'

'Godfrey? That's going to be difficult.'

'Why is that difficult?'

'Well, he's gone incommunicado. I don't just walk up to these people. I don't know where they are.'

'You need to find him,' said Kirsten. 'You need to find him and then I'll meet you in Inverness. I have a short trip to Aberdeen and then back.'

'Okay. Anything else I can do for you?'

'I need you to contact Detective Lumley at Stornoway police station. See if you can get a safe house set up for someone. Lumley's going to join her though. Insist upon it.'

'Why?' asked Craig.

'Just do it for me, please. I need to think about things.'

'Are you okay, Kirsten?' he asked.

'Of course, I'm not. They just told me we suspect Anna Hunt as a traitor. I'm trying to find out if she is or not. It's scrambling my head. Meet me in Inverness, two days' time. Just join us up at the headquarters. You'll look less conspicuous that way. Anyone that knows you will know you're there for a good reason. If we meet out and about, they might suspect a lot more.'

'I might suspect a lot more. I barely know what's going on.'

'Welcome to the club,' said Kirsten. 'Welcome to the club,' and she closed the call.

'You're none the wiser about him,' said Dom.

'No,' said Kirsten. 'We didn't get all the details, Dom, and

I'm not happy about it. He says he can't get Godfrey at the moment. Godfrey's not about.'

'Convenient,' said Dom. 'So what? We just keep her alive until?'

'We go to Aberdeen, and we see what happens. If Anna's left these notes, she wants help.'

'Or she set us onto a trap. You can't read her mind. I don't think, I don't want to think that she's jumped ship,' said Dom, 'but don't read her mind. She's too clever for that.'

'You're not wrong there,' said Kirsten. She put her phone away, turned on the ignition, and drove off into the town.

Chapter 14

Kirsten and Dom took the ferry across the Minch, the body of water between Lewis and the mainland, over to the west side of Scotland. From Ullapool, they returned to Inverness and met up with Carrie Anne and Justin. Together the four of them travelled across to Aberdeen, making a direct line to the amusement park that sat up by the coast. It was a large place, with bowling, restaurants as well as the amusement park, and also a small mini-golf course.

Rather than all race to the Waltzer, Kirsten had the three of them scout around. Justin was left camped up in a small hotel, running comms from a distance. Carrie Anne had said how he'd reacted when she'd had to take out the three men around him and Kirsten was worried that this could be a similar situation.

She didn't quite know what she was walking into. She hoped this would be Anna looking for help, but it could be Anna having organised a trap. Somewhere to finish off her would-be assassins. Had anyone followed them?

She trusted Detective Lumley to do the right thing, but on the other hand, it wouldn't be that difficult to go and have a word with Linda. If somebody official turned up, it'd be hard for Lumley to protect her and then they would have to tell. They always knew when you were lying, the people who were really good at this, and they would extract the information somehow. Kirsten could only hope that she was right in her gut feeling that Anna wasn't a traitor and secondly, quick enough so that others would not be on her tail when she made the connection. She also wondered if Craig would meet with Godfrey. Could he get through to him? She'd know in a day or so when she went back to Inverness to meet him.

As Kirsten walked past some arcades, she saw Dom about one hundred yards away, strolling beside a merry-go-round, giving a little shake of his head. She walked past the candy floss stall. Carrie Anne gave a wag of her finger, never looking at Kirsten once. It seemed like the place may be clean, though Kirsten would never take that for granted.

Inside her jacket was stowed her weapon, though she didn't want to use it in a place like this, so public. She understood Carrie Anne's reaction when she took out the three men who were holding Justin but in there the only people who could get injured were Justin, herself, and the three people she had to kill. Here amongst the general populace, a stray shot could take out someone, anyone, and those who didn't really care about what the service stood for, or were from other parts, would not be that worried who they took out.

Kirsten looked up at the Waltzer and saw the gaudy colours of the lights shining even though it was daylight. She looked at the swirling colours with fancy women looking like they were out for a night on the town, men with chiselled chins, sharp and effectively gorgeous, there ready to entertain the women. She wondered how these rides kept on producing this type of motif. Surely people didn't fall for that. They didn't think these things were appropriate these days.

Then she looked down, saw the cars going round, spinning. The floor moved up and down as the car spun. Kirsten could remember being a child on them, feeling sick to her core. However, she made her way forward and stood waiting for the light to stop.

When it did, she marched forward to take one of the cars, but two kids jumped in in front of her when clearly, she had reached it first. She wanted to give them a good clip around the ear, but instead, not wanting to cause a scene, she moved on round until she found a car on her own. As she sat there, two youths came up to her, maybe eighteen or nineteen. She saw one turn to the other, pointing at her. There was a brief discussion.

'You don't mind if we sit here, do you?' said one of the boys.

Kirsten could see what was going on. If she had been seventeen, she might have been flattered, but she was on business and she thought about the possibilities of what could happen.

'Sorry, lads. Single ride only.'

One of the boys punched the other on the arm. 'Hot as,' he said, turning away. Kirsten shook her head, almost laughing at the teens before she reached forward and pulled the single bar across the cab. A man came round taking money and after she had paid, Kirsten waited until the ride began.

At first her cab swung round lightly, the weak up and down motion not meaning she felt much, but then the cab began to spin and she realised there was a rotund woman swinging the cab for her. There was a smile on the woman's face. She tried to look past her, seeing if she could spot Anna anywhere around the ride, but the woman kept smiling and spinning. Kirsten found herself dazed as it went round and round so quickly. Then Kirsten heard the words, 'I'm in trouble. Require your assistance.'

Kirsten gripped the bar, but she couldn't move because the cab was spinning so hard.

'When the ride's over, come round the back of it,' said the voice. 'I can tell you some more.'

The car continued to spin. Kirsten saw the rotund woman waddling away, moving to the next cab and spinning it. She came past twice more, spinning the cab Kirsten was sitting in before the ride ended. By the time Kirsten got out, the woman was not to be seen.

Kirsten stepped off the ride, touched her nose with her hand, indicating to her team that she'd found her quarry. She quickly walked round to the back of the ride, realising that part of it was hemmed in and couldn't be approached. There was a caravan back there. Kirsten opened the door and walked in.

'So, you got it then. I thought you would eventually. Justin tell you where to look?'

'We did.'

'How did you know I was in trouble?' asked Anna. 'You wouldn't have heard from me, but then that's not that uncommon.'

'I didn't hear you were in trouble; I was told you were the trouble,' said Kirsten. 'I was told to find you and kill you.'

'Well,' said Anna, 'I'm standing right here. You've had your orders, haven't you?'

'From a Control I don't know. I thought I should let you have a chance to explain what's going on.'

'I take it Linda gave you the message then. Or should I say Orla?'

'You should say Linda,' said Kirsten quickly. 'She's got a broken leg and they smashed her face. Tortured her with fag butts, the lot, but she never gave up any information.'

'No, she couldn't,' said Anna, almost dispassionately.

'Don't you care? She's in a bad way.'

'She was going to be in a bad way, whatever happened. They were going to come and look for her. I was hoping you might get to her first, but I couldn't really call you to tell you.'

'Why?' asked Kirsten.

'Because they're all over you. They've been all over you the day it happened to me. I'm being set up. You need to understand that, Kirsten. I'm being set up because I know something they don't want me to know.'

'We've got a friendly onsite,' said a voice in Kirsten's ear.

'Confirm, friendly.'

'Friendly as we know, I don't know who's friendly and who isn't anymore,' said Dom. 'It's your man from London, the driver.'

'Where is he?' asked Kirsten.

'He's making his way towards the Waltzer.'

Kirsten heart skipped a beat. What was he doing here? He was told to meet her in Inverness. He was also in North Berwick.

'You need to level with me, Anna, and fast. Carrie Anne had to put three people down. Someone else was put down in front of her in North Berwick. Everywhere we go people are getting hurt. I'm being told you're the problem and I have to eliminate you. Yet there's all these other people running around. What I have noticed is none of them seem to be batting for you, at least as far as I can tell.'

'You said you got your information from Control. What did

Control look like?'

'You're leaving me in a quandary, Anna. You're not telling me much from your side,' said Kirsten. 'I've got friendlies here coming towards.'

'Friendlies? You're on a kill order. You should be dark, why are the friendlies around? They're following you. You don't get followed on a kill order. Use your brain.'

'You help me use it. Tell me what's going on?'

'Tell me about Control first. Who was it?'

Kirsten kept quiet.

'He's at the Waltzer,' said Dom, over the comms. 'Friendly at Waltzer.'

'There's someone outside coming soon,' said Kirsten. 'Talk to me.'

'Bald,' said Anna. 'She was bald, wasn't she?' Kirsten tried not to give anything away, but Anna clicked her fingers. 'That's it, of course. Someone from outside. Clean up. They're worried about being dirtied. Listen, it's all to do with this data stick. I was told a piece of information. It's on a scrap of paper here. I wanted to give it to you, Kirsten. You need to have it, but you take this, and you'll become the hunted. Do you understand me? This is why they're after me. If they know you've got it, they'll come after you.'

'What does that mean?' asked Kirsten. 'Who do we give it to? Who's going to use this?'

'I don't know,' said Anna. 'I really don't.'

'Friendly moving round. He's coming your way. If you don't want to be seen, you should get down.'

'It's all a bit rich to swallow, Anna. They're coming after you for a piece of information you don't even know how to use.'

'It does happen,' said Anna. 'It does. Who's talking in your ear? What are they telling you? Is it Dom? Is Dom speaking to you? Is he okay? Do you trust the rest of them?'

'I brought them with me, didn't I?'

'Not Justin though,' said Anna. 'Didn't see Justin out there.'

'Justin's running comms at a distance. He's not that good in the field, is he? What does the message mean? What is it about?' asked Kirsten.

'I told you, I don't know.'

'Approaching the door,' said Dom. 'Friendly is approaching the door.' Kirsten reached down for her weapon, taking it in hand. She then heard a cry. It was Craig's voice outside. There was the sound of gunfire and the window of the caravan shattered. Kirsten saw Anna spin and fall to the ground. Kirsten hit the floor of the caravan as a second window blew out.

Chapter 15

'Where's that gun coming from, Dom?' Kirsten yelled into her mouthpiece, while lying on the floor of the caravan. Another window was shot out and she saw Anna beginning to scramble across the floor. 'No, you don't. You're not going anywhere.'

'We need to get out,' said Anna. 'Out.' Kirsten could see the trail of blood as Anna dragged herself across the floor.

'You're not in a state to go anywhere.'

'You tell that to that gunman. We've got to move.'

'Charlie,' came a voice across the airwaves. 'Your three o'clock. Twenty metres, can you see him?'

'Delta. Got it.' There were more shots from outside, and Kirsten pulled herself up on her knees backing herself up against the wall of the caravan and moved over towards the door. She had the gun pointed upright, waiting for anyone to come in.

'Charlie. Gunman down.'

'Kilo, this is Delta. Coming in now.' Kirsten kept her gun focused on the door, then saw it open and Dom step inside. She peered out, but only saw a panicking public running here, there, and everywhere.

No, thought Kirsten, *this is a right mess*. 'Charlie, we need to extract. Are we clear to remove from the caravan?' said Kirsten, through her earpiece.

'Negative. Negative. Hold position.' Kirsten saw Carrie Anne running across in front of the caravan then moving in behind one of the other rides. She saw the woman discharge her weapon twice before running through again. 'Kilo, you're good to go. Good to go.'

Kirsten looked over at Dom, who was reaching down to Anna Hunt. 'Restrain her,' said Kirsten.

'Restrain her?' asked Dom. 'She can barely bloody move. It's hit the shoulder; she's bleeding. We need to get her somewhere to get treatment.'

'Keep an eye.'

'She's right,' Anna said to Dom. 'You should treat me with extreme prejudice; you have no idea what I'm involved in.'

'I don't need to be babysat by either of you,' said Dom. 'Clear the way please, boss.' Kirsten gave him a nod, stepped out of the caravan, and then ducked back in as a shot ricocheted off the top of the caravan roof.

'Got him,' said Carrie Anne on the earpiece, and she moved off, Kirsten watching the woman sprinting through the rides.

'I think we should split, Dom,' Kirsten said to him. 'I'll go out, head off through the Waltzer. You make your way out the back, I'll find you, but head south 'cause they'll expect us to head back for Inverness.'

Dom nodded and took Anna's arm, putting it around his neck. Kirsten sped out of the caravan and ran in behind the Waltzer.

'I think we've got two here,' said Carrie Anne. 'One moving onto the Waltzer at the moment, heading for the caravan.'

'I've got him,' said Kirsten. 'Keep the route out from the Waltzer clear. How many more do you think there are?'

'I'm not even sure how many sides are here. Charlie, how many?'

'Four to five, six, seven. Something like that. Just don't get out in the open. Stay in cover.'

Kirsten moved into the Waltzer, hiding behind one of the cars. There were mirrors on the inside, and she scanned them looking for any reflection, any movement. Suddenly someone stood up and made a run for it. Kirsten stood up from behind her car, gun pointed at the person but then realised it was a lad of about fifteen making his way out. She quickly ducked down and heard a bullet rattle into the car she was behind. Someone was up here. She felt pinned down, not able to go either side of the car.

'Delta, are you clear?' she said.

'Making my way out.'

'Charlie, I'm pinned, can you help?'

'Pinned myself. There's too many of them, Kilo.'

Kirsten pushed the car around slightly, making sure she had the maximum cover from it, keeping down low behind it. The circular bend of the car allowed her to peer to the edge without exposing her head. She saw a man in the mirror starting to move towards her. He was working towards the outside of the ride, so she stepped to the inside middle where she saw the large control panel.

'Kilo, you've got a second joining you, and a third.'

Kirsten started the ride up; she wasn't going to be pinned down. If things were moving, she'd have more chance, especially with three of them. She'd need to trust her instincts, trust her reactions. As the ride began to move, she stepped out into one of the cars, her head peering across the top. She saw a figure on the far side coming round with the ride. One was still on the outside looking in, and she tried to ensure that the car was always spinning, holding the larger side of it to the outside, but where was the third?

Kirsten heard a shot pummel into her car again, and this time as the ride moved up and down, she stepped off, trying to maintain her balance before throwing herself into the middle. Everything spun around her, and as she stepped up, the man who had been targeting her before spun past in his car. She fired one shot, saw him tumble, and as the car spun around, part of him fell out of it. The glass above her broke as a shot from outside the Waltzer exploded a small toy chandelier.

Keep your damn head down, Kirsten, she said to herself and started scanning the ride for the third person. She'd need to get clear soon, as the police would be on their way. Soon, the park would be crawling with all sorts of authority.

As Kirsten tried to slowly edge around the centre, she heard a noise behind her and instantly dropped. Hearing a gunshot go past her, she swept her leg out behind connecting with someone who then fell to the ground.

Kirsten spun around and dove for the gun, managing to get two hands on a wrist and drive it down onto the floor. It was a blonde-haired woman who hit her with a punch to the face. The blow was surprisingly good, but Kirsten hung on as hard as she could. She was used to taking a punch, used to pulling herself together to keep going. The woman was strong, but Kirsten left one hand on her wrist and grabbed the woman's shoulder with her other hand.

She spun over as hard as she could, taking the woman out onto the rising and falling track of the Waltzer. Kirsten was shorter than her, and she allowed herself to slip down the woman's figure. Her head was up to the woman's chest. The woman reached down with a hand, grabbing Kirsten's throat, and the hold was strong. Kirsten was biding her time, waiting for that moment. She rolled over again. One of the cars spun round colliding with the woman's head, causing her to cry out and release Kirsten's hands.

Kirsten rolled on top of the woman whose eyes seem to be unfocused, but she delivered two more punches before standing up. She ran down the Waltzer, jumping onto the platform at the edge but hiding behind one of the structures. There was still someone outside. As she waited, the woman who had attacked her rolled, eventually coming down to rest just across from Kirsten. She was clearly out cold, but a figure from outside moved towards her.

Kirsten stepped out from her cover, grabbed this man by the shoulder and hair, and drove his head in towards one of the cars as they came around. She didn't wait to see the effect, but ran out from the Waltzer, and then behind a candy floss van. 'Charlie, are you clear?' Kirsten cried across the comms.

'Just a minute,' Carrie Anne replied. 'Delta, are you clear?'

'Delta is clear with target. Call for rendezvous.'

'Kilo, Charlie coming to your assistance.' The comms line remained open, and Kirsten heard a loud thud. For a moment her heart jumped. 'Kilo, Your way is clear. I have been compromised. Charlie clear, call for rendezvous. See ya.'

Kirsten understood what it meant—authorities were arriving, and she pocketed her gun. As she ran to the side of the amusement park, there were people running around screaming and shouting, and she saw a young boy had fallen on the ground. He was bleeding from his mouth, probably caught in a trample. Kirsten picked him up and carried him out of the gate. Policemen ran in, but Kirsten, clearly concerned about the boy, walked past them, and to an ambulance.

The medic looked at her. 'What happened to him?'

'I don't know. I'm not his mum. He just fell down, I think. Here. You've got him now.' The paramedic grabbed the boy and took him inside the back of the ambulance.

'Are you going to remain?' The paramedic looked around and Kirsten was gone.

And though she was clear of the amusement park, from the possible people who'd been coming to kill her or Anna, Kirsten's guard was not let up. She had felt her phone vibrating, but she didn't touch it knowing it would probably be Justin. That could wait. She needed to make sure she was clear. She paced down the street in the opposite direction from other people who seem to be running towards the chaos.

Kirsten never understood what made people do this. There'd been gunfire. There were ambulance and police services, but everyone wanted a view. Generally, that wasn't a good thing. Who knew if the gunfire was over? She always thought the people who lived in real war zones, or places where terrorism had gone on a long time, always seemed wiser. They just left the area.

Kirsten spotted a taxi, ran and jumped in the back of the cab, telling the driver to take her to a train station. As he sped through the streets of Aberdeen, Kirsten tried to relax, then realised that she was bleeding just under her nose.

'You all right, love?' the man asked.

'You haven't got a tissue, have you?' she said. 'Bloody nose bleeds, eh.'

The man reached forward in his cab, and through the hole

in the wall between himself and the passenger area, he passed a tissue. Kirsten folded it up, shoved it up her nose, and held it

'I don't think I've bled on your car.'

'What's all the commotion up there?'

'Commotion? I don't know. I'm just in a bit of a hurry to catch the train. I suppose that's what brought the nosebleed on—sick of these things happening,' said Kirsten, and again the phone vibrated in her pocket.

This time she pulled it out and saw Justin's face on the call. She didn't answer it, instead pressing the text message button typing in two words: *rendezvous delta*. Dom would decide where they would meet, and they would each have to contact him using a single prepaid phone SIM card. They would get an address, and nothing else, and then have to make their way there. Kirsten had told them to go south since Dom would go to the station and grab a train.

'There you are,' said the taxi driver. Kirsten reached in her pocket, pulling out a tenner, and passed it through the window.

'Just keep the change.'

'Thanks very much.'

'You take care, love,' said the man. 'You may want to go get looked at by a doctor. Seemed to bleed quite a bit.'

'It's just normal,' said Kirsten. 'Not to worry.'

She left the taxi, entering the train station and heading directly for the women's toilets. Once inside, she checked; no one was there, and she took a look at her nose. The tissue had done well, and the blood was starting to clot, but it was sitting just at the bottom of her nose. Kirsten reached up with her hands. They started to tremble.

What was this heat? Where was it coming from? Someone just took a pot shot at Anna Hunt. This was Anna. The woman was tight with what she did. People didn't get to take shots at Anna. When she had steadied herself, Kirsten made her way onto the platform and looked up at the screen. She'd be on a train and heading for Montrose in approximately twenty minutes.

She bought herself a coffee and sat with a sandwich as if nothing else mattered in the day. After boarding the train, she sat at peace watching the world go by but keeping a distinct eye on her cabin for any untoward travellers. When she stepped off at Montrose, she felt a lot happier.

Kirsten found a B&B, paid cash, and took up a room. *I'm dead for the afternoon*, she thought. She needed to give time for Dom to get somewhere, but he could need her help soon. After she had rested for three hours, she looked inside her jacket, took out a SIM card, placed it in her phone and made the call. She was delighted to hear Dom's voice and he gave a street and a house number, followed by a postcode.

Kirsten looked up the map on her phone and saw that Dom was actually on the other side of Montrose. Having cleaned up her wound, Kirsten left the B&B and walked the whole way across town, not wanting a taxi driver to have any idea where she'd been. When she came to the address, it was a disused former factory, and she could see the broken windows at the top of the building. She didn't open the door but instead walked into the alley at the back.

From there, she could see a broken window a floor up, and using a drainpipe, she climbed up, carefully finding her way through the cut glass. Once inside, she saw a floor with redundant machinery, bits and pieces, as if a lot of it had been stripped. She climbed to the second floor, and as she walked across the hall, she got the distinct feeling she was being watched. She turned to her right and saw Carrie Anne standing with a gun.

'You made it. Good,' said Carrie Anne. 'Dom's through there with Anna. There's also a doctor, so watch what you say.'

Kirsten went to walk into the room, but she felt her phone vibrating again. Picking it up, she saw it was a call from Craig. She closed the call down without answering it and switched her mobile phone off. Stepping inside, she saw Anna stretched out on a make-shift table, her arm lying out to one side with the doctor over it. Kirsten wasn't quite sure what he was doing, but there was a good deal of blood around her. She also saw a pack of blood hanging up with tubes going into Anna.

'Delta, what's the report?' said Kirsten, knowing not to use any names in front of the doctor.

'She's going to be okay,' said Dom. 'He'll only be a few more minutes, he says, but she's going to need to take it easy. She lost a lot of blood. He's going to come back a few times.'

'Is he okay? How do you know him?'

'He's patched me up on many an occasion; don't worry. He's going in and out in the hood, then we're going to drop him away from here in case he gets picked up.'

'Does anybody know you know him?' asked Kirsten.

'Easy, boss. I've been at this a long time. Nobody knows him, and refer to him as Doc, only Doc, okay?'

Kirsten nodded and stood by Anna, watching the doctor finish patching up her wounds. Anna rolled over, and looked up.

'A bit of a mess, then,' she said. 'But you found me, and you found her as well.' The conversation was coded because of the doctor, and Kirsten simply nodded.

'She's safe' said Kirsten. 'Let's have the doc fix you up first.

Once he's done, we need to talk.'

Anna gave Kirsten a smile. Kirsten wasn't ready to return; not yet. The whole thing was a mess; there'd been a fire fight in the amusement park. People would wonder what was going on. Of course, it would get covered up to some degree. They'd say it was a drug war or something happening like that. Kirsten's patience was running out. All that was going on, all the violence and death surrounding Anna, and still Kirsten had no idea what the truth of the situation was.

Chapter 16

Kirsten stood in the hallway of the building and watched Dom take the Doc out of the makeshift treatment room. He brought him across to Kirsten who gave the man a smile.

'Thanks for that, Doc. Dom says you're good at this, so how much more will you need to come back?'

The man had a gruff accent, born somewhere in the high-lands. He gave a wry smile.

'She really should be in a hospital. She's lost a lot of blood. I'm going to come back probably two or three times and give her some more blood. Make sure her levels are okay. It'll take time to get on her feet. This is not exactly an ideal place. I've told my man here that she'll need to stay warm, blankets and stuff. Probably best if you move her into a proper house, if you have something like that. Any issues, he can reach me. He knows.'

'Okay,' said Kirsten, 'but I'm okay to talk to her though, aren't I?'

'Oh, she's lucid. She'll be tired, but she's lucid.'

Kirsten nodded. 'Dom, put a hood over the doctor's head. Thanks again, Doc,' said Kirsten, and made her way into the room with Anna. She took her gun into her hand, making sure Anna saw it, and asked Carrie Anne to leave the room. 'Just stay outside. Make sure no one's poking about. Justin should be arriving as well. Thought I heard Dom taking a call from him.'

Carrie Anne nodded and looked over at Anna Hunt. Kirsten could see Carrie Anne's face was dubious, unsure of her boss.

'I'll be outside if you need me,' said Carrie Anne. Quietly, she left the room.

'You've got a gun with you,' said Anna. 'I'm shot. I was bleeding out until that good doctor helped me and I'm a little bit tired. I don't think you'll need it.'

'I don't know what I'll need at the moment,' said Kirsten. 'You're a quandary, a mystery. I've been chasing around after you. Your sister was beat to pieces and was dumped in a car to go over a cliff before I pulled her out, and I don't even know the sides that are following you. I got handed a kill order, a no-questions-kill order.'

'Yet, here you are asking questions,' said Anna. 'I knew you weren't just a mindless drone. Macleod was right when he filled in his forms about you. He said she can think; he said she had a mind.'

'The mind is wondering what's going on, Anna. Am I out on a limb?'

'No, you're not,' said Anna. 'So far you've been involved in a few fire fights looking for me. You've pulled me out to one side. You haven't put a bullet in me yet, but if you do, you can walk back to Control and say, "She's dead. We got her. What was all the heat on me?" They can't throw anything else at you.'

'No, but they could take me aside and put a bullet in me. Why are they wanting you? What have you done? What have you done that justifies a bullet and not being brought in and interrogated?'

'You need to ask the question who wants to put a bullet in me?'

'Well, yes. I need to ask the question who's actually involved to begin with, never mind work out who's actually putting a bullet in you.'

'I don't actually know, but that piece of paper I gave you—it's important.'

Kirsten pulled out the paper from inside her jacket. She'd looked at it on the train, but it meant nothing to her. 'It's got coordinates. Why didn't you just go to the coordinates?' asked Kirsten.

'Because they're not simple coordinates. It's not a latitude and a longitude. They're coded. They're the answer to what you're seeking. Wherever that is, whatever's there has meant that people are hunting me for that piece of paper.'

'You don't know what it is?'

'I tried to take it to Godfrey because he would know what to do with it, but before I could get near him, suddenly people were after me, so I went dark. Trouble is Godfrey's not that simple to get hold of. The higher up you get in this organisation, the more difficult it is to stay dark. You've got it quite easy really, Kirsten, and you can do it quite well. How many people really know you? Godfrey's known. It's not so easy for him to be out on the loose. People follow where he is. Take our driver down in London, always looking out for Godfrey. Godfrey has protection around him. Godfrey doesn't pitch up in the dark all alone. That's for the likes of you, occasionally for the likes of me, but that note needs to get to Godfrey.'

'Why? What's he going to do with it? You told me that they were coordinates, but they're coded.'

'Godfrey will know how to decode them. He has people with certain books. He has certain contacts, things you don't let out, things people don't need to know. It's the other reason why I can't just simply pitch up, but they're coming,' said Anna. 'They're coming in their droves.'

'Who's coming?' asked Kirsten.

'Control. You said Control gave you the mission. Bald-headed woman? Not from our service. How do you know she's from any service?'

'She knew who I was.'

'Lots of people know who you are in other services. Information gets leaked. Oh, they don't run around dispatching people. After all, you work here, don't you? You're within the country. You're not working out in other countries. If you did, you'd be on their watch list coming into the country. Then they'd kill you. You're a spy, but you're a spy on the inside, within our country. Frankly, they couldn't give a damn. They could go around killing you, but why? Better to know who you are in case they get seen by you or they see you near them.'

'So, they'll know who you are as well, yet they seem to want to kill you.'

'Because of that, that paper. Now you've got me. Unfortunately, Aberdeen was a bit public. I was hoping by getting to the Waltzer that you could get me on my own. I could pass you the information, then you'd be clear to walk about, maybe even stroll to Godfrey. Not now. Now your whole team is going to be hunted down. I'm quite worried that Justin's not here yet.'

'He'll be here. This side of things he can handle, staying on his own, out of the way.'

'But they would trace him from the Inverness office.'

'He is not in the Inverness office,' said Kirsten. 'He coming in from remote, so if he gets here, it'll be okay.'

'You need to go dark,' said Anna. 'You need to go dark and you need to find out what that piece of paper is. You need to get it to Godfrey.'

'I'm meant to do all this on trust. But, this is important?'

'It's important enough that they want to kill me for it. Look, Kirsten, you're shrewd, and I don't expect you to trust me and I expect you to follow what's in front of you. Godfrey is near the top of our organisation. He's sound, that's why I wanted to go to him. There are others in the path up I don't trust. Some of them just because I'm a suspicious type of sod, but others because I have my doubts. I have no doubts about Godfrey, but you need to get it to him on the quiet.'

'And he is where?'

'Not easy to find. He doesn't do public dates. He's not the queen, but Justin's the one for that. Justin has connections you don't know about. He'll find you things and he never tells you where they come from. He's thick within our organisation, but he also needs protecting. He's not as sharp as you, or Carrie Anne, or Dom. He's not a field agent.' Kirsten heard a noise outside, and the door to the room opened with Carrie Anne apologising.

'Sorry, boss, but Justin's here, wanted to know if you wanted to see him straight away.'

'How is he?' asked Kirsten.

'Shook up. Said when he left his building, he was tailed, shook them off.'

'Do a sweep outside, Carrie Anne. Make sure we're not

being looked at. I'll come out and see Justin now.' Carrie Anne nodded, and Kirsten left Anna, wondering just how trustworthy the woman was. She switched her phone back on to see if anyone was trying to contact her.

As she entered the hall outside, she saw Justin shaking. 'It's all got a bit crazy, hasn't it?' he said.

'As long as you're here, we got work to do but I'll brief you when the rest come back.'

'I had two different people tailing me,' he said. 'I shook them both, but there were two different people.'

'Yes,' said Kirsten. 'There were two different groups of people at the fairground as well, at least. Might be a third group. Anna took a bullet from someone.'

'Do you mind if I see her?' Justin asked.

'I do. For now, she speaks through me. Nobody else talks about anything with her. The only thing you discuss with her is whether she needs food and water or if she's sore. Nothing else.'

'I could let her know her sister's okay.'

'No, Justin. I've already spoken with her about it. How is Linda anyway?'

'The last call I placed, she seemed to be doing okay.'

'Good,' said Kirsten. 'As of now, we're going dark, properly dark.' Her phone vibrated again. Kirsten took it out, seeing it was Craig. She didn't want to speak to him, but inside, she knew she had to understand what parties were involved. Craig was, and he was a party that she might be able to talk to as opposed to simply hide from, but he'd been there at the caravan. Had he been responsible for any shots? He disappeared as well, quickly, when everything had gone south.

Kirsten found a corner and sat down. Things were too

complicated. She needed a way out. She needed to start getting on the offensive, find out what was going on.

'Justin,' she shouted across, 'Godfrey.' Justin's eyebrows raised. 'Find me Godfrey. Find me his schedule and do it quietly. No one can know where we are, but find me Godfrey.'

Justin nodded. Kirsten could see the man was on edge.

Carrie Anne approached. 'Sweep concluded. There's nobody out there. Nobody knows we're here.'

'Good. Tell Dom when he comes back, we're dark, proper dark. Nobody needs to know where we are. Anna's got a piece of paper with coordinates on it that are coded. We need to get to Godfrey.'

'Who's Godfrey?' asked Carrie Anne.

'One of the people at the top of the organisation. Met him once. Anna says he can provide us with a reason why this piece of paper is important.'

'Where did she get it?' asked Carrie Anne.

'She hasn't said so far. I don't think she wants to. She'd be compromising someone.'

'I think she's worried it'd go south and we get caught with it. They could interrogate it out of us.'

'That's what I think. Well, I don't know. It's like I don't know her, Carrie.'

'I don't like this,' said Carrie Anne. 'We operate in the dark. We're getting pulled here and there for somebody else's actions. We need to understand what's happening.'

'I got a call from Craig.'

'Craig?' asked Carrie Anne.

'The driver, the one down in London. I'm going to meet him, get to the bottom what his role is. It's a couple of times he's shown up.'

Carrie Anne nodded. 'Time to go on the offensive, boss.' she said. 'You're right. Time to go on the offensive.'

Chapter 17

Kirsten was in a dilemma about who to trust so she decided to play her boyfriend to see what side he was on. Clearly, everyone wanted something that Anna had, and she wondered how many people knew what it was. She got Justin to make up some sheets detailing a particular weapon. They were not completely accurate, but if somebody had a quick scan at them, they would believe that they were detailed documents before passing them onto a proper engineer.

Having had Justin produce these, she then photographed them, put them onto a small SD card which she placed in an envelope. Using a pay-as-you-go SIM card, she messaged Craig advising she had got from Anna what she had been carrying and needed to give it back to Control. She also stated she was still in the Aberdeen area and that she had dropped the parcel at a location in Aberdeen before messaging him with the details so he could pick it up.

Craig messaged back asking about detail on Anna's current status. Kirsten replied that she was deceased. She wasn't sure if he would believe her or not, but she was doing what was necessary. When he messaged back asking why she wouldn't just come in herself she advised that other parties had been involved and she didn't want to break cover at this time until she was sure they were away. She got an okay in return advising that he was waiting for her next text.

Kirsten told the team that they would wait with Anna, and to try and secure a better location, somewhere a bit more salubrious for all of them. Having given the message to protect Anna and move her if necessary, she reiterated to Justin that he needed to get her contact with Godfrey, Anna's high-up contact in the services.

Within the hour, Kirsten returned to Montrose Railway Station and took the short trip up the coast to Aberdeen. Arriving at the platforms, she strode out into the conurbation known as the Granite City. She scoured the edge of the train station and when she could see no one there, she returned inside and picked her locker.

She pressed in the code to open it, paying for a two day stay, and dropped a simple envelope inside, before closing the door. She adjusted the code, turned around, and then left, disappearing into the lady's toilets to put on a disguise. She messaged Craig advising the location of the package before quickly making herself up to look like a much older woman. A grey-powdered wig, the long skirt with boots underneath all covered over with a large jacket.

She still had her rucksack which she believed looked old enough, so that it was still in character. Then she walked to the coffee shop from where she could watch the lockers. Instead of ordering coffee, she took tea and she settled back with a novel in front of her. It was one of those romantic novels that filled every station kiosk, but Kirsten wasn't reading it despite the fact that the page turned approximately every minute.

It took an hour and a half before she saw Craig approaching. He was wearing a suit and made his way directly to the locker where he punched in the code. Kirsten drank the last of her tea, stood up, and strode out of the building following on Craig's tail. He hailed a cab, got inside, and she watched him drive off before hailing a cab herself.

'That's my son,' she said. 'Can you follow him? I don't want to alarm him, but I think he's getting confused again. Can we just keep a tail behind?'

'I could try and talk to the taxi in front if you want, ma'am,' said the taxi driver.

'No, no. It's just, he has issues. We just need to keep a distance. If he goes to the wrong place, I'll get out and talk to him.' The taxi driver looked at her strangely, shook his shoulders, and drove off after the other taxi.

'I can pull up just alongside at the lights. We could roll the windows down. You could talk to him then,' said the taxi driver.

'No, he can become violent if he's surprised. Really, it's best we just hang back,' said Kirsten in a croaky voice.

'Well, it's your money,' said the taxi driver. 'I take it you've got enough to cover this.'

'I do indeed, young man,' said Kirsten, indignant, and she slapped forty pounds through the gap in the taxi driver's window.

'Well, you're the boss, then. Following we do.'

Craig's taxi drove out of Aberdeen into the countryside before turning down a narrow lane at the end of which a sign indicated was a countryside walk. Kirsten's taxi continued to follow until she saw it reach the car park, and she demanded that the driver stop.

'He is in the wrong place,' she said. 'We'd better just be on the safe side. Stop here, please.' Kirsten got out of the taxi but the taxi driver rapped the window at her.

'Do you want me to wait, love?'

'No, I'll be fine. This might take a wee while.'

'If he gets violent, I can be here for you. I don't mind waiting. I mean, you're paying.'

'No, no,' said Kirsten. 'Honestly, it's not a bother.'

Kirsten wandered off down the path until the taxi had disappeared before jumping into the hedge beside the road. From there, she shed her wig and her clothing and felt better back in her jeans and leather jacket. She kept the rucksack slung over her back, packing the other clothing into it. Once she had it all together, she put the rucksack on her back, and quickly made her way down to the car park.

There were several cars sitting inside, most of them empty but one had a man sitting in the front seat. He seemed to be in a shirt and tie. This gave Kirsten cause for concern, but she couldn't see Craig. She skirted the edge of the car park, keeping in behind the trees so no one could see her, and then crept down one of the country paths. There was one that seemed quite open, running along the side of a field. She disregarded that one to take the one that headed up into the thick wood and paced quickly along. She could hear talking up ahead and ducked in behind some trees, deciding instead to start routing beside the path, parallel to it, in the denser vegetation. As she got closer to the voices, she stopped and crouched down.

'And this is all she had for you? This envelope with this card inside?' Kirsten peered from behind a tree. It was the bald-headed woman, Control.

'That's all that was there. Nothing else.'

'You checked the whole locker?'

'Yes.'

'Have you looked to see what's on this?'

'Of course, I haven't,' said Craig. 'I was told to pick it up, so I have, and I've brought it to you.'

'Just a moment,' said the woman. She pulled a laptop out of her bag. Kirsten watched as she put the SD card in, punched a few buttons, no doubt looking at the contents of the files.

'And this is all she gave you, all that was left?'

'That's all,' said Craig. Kirsten saw the woman nod, close her laptop, and shout over.

'Allan, you can come back now.' A six-foot-four man built like a tank appeared from up the path. 'Thank you for your help, Craig, but I think you've been played.'

'Well, if I have been, I don't quite understand why. I still don't understand why there was such weapons' fire at the amusement park. I was told it would be simple, just to check up that Anna was really dead. You think she's still out there?'

'I fear you're asking too many questions,' said the bald-headed woman. 'You've done what's been asked. Simply go back, take up your old job, and remember, tell no one about this.'

'Of course not. I'm fully vetted.'

'So was Anna Hunt,' said Control. Craig nodded and turned away and Kirsten could see that his face was full of worry and confusion. Was he wondering why Kirsten had given him the wrong things? Was he worried at Control? His shoulders were slumped, and he shuffled off down the path, back towards the car park.

Couched in the undergrowth, Kirsten felt for Craig, and she wondered just what his part was in all of this. He said he'd been there to make sure Anna was dead, but there was gunfire coming in from all quarters and he hadn't been there when she came out of the caravan. Where had he gone? What had he been organising?

As she watched him, part of her wanted to go to him, to shake him and find out what was happening. She wanted to believe that he was just getting played along as well, that maybe his side was the clean side and had just misunderstood Anna, but she had to be careful.

She'd been given a kill order. There would be no tiptoeing around what was happening. If they found Anna, they'd dispatch her, and Anna already said that if Kirsten and her team are seen out and about now, any side would dispatch them. Kirsten glanced back at Control and her bodyguard, saw them packing up their bags and begin to follow Craig down the path.

Control turned to her bodyguard, gave a nod, and Kirsten saw him begin to take out his gun from within his jacket. They were both facing forward looking at Craig's rear. There was only one thing that nod could mean. Kirsten put her head down and broke cover from the vegetation running for all she was worth at the hand of the bodyguard which now held his weapon, and which was pointing at Craig's back. She had to be quick, or Craig would be dead.

Chapter 18

Kirsten leapt from the undergrowth throwing herself with all her might at the bodyguard and smacked into his arm just as he fired the weapon. There was no loud retort for the weapon was silenced, but the man clattered to the ground catching Control at the same time. She tumbled over as well. Kirsten tried to roll, but with her backpack on it made it difficult and she ended up having to spring back to her feet. As the large bodyguard got to his feet, he stood in line with the path preventing her from getting to Craig and stepped forward.

He threw a punch with his left hand, but she dodged, followed by another with his right, but then he faked with his left and she put up a block before realising that the right was the one she should have been watching. The punch caught her square in the jaw.

Kirsten fell back hard. Thankfully the man's gun had fallen to the floor and he bent over her, both hands outstretched for her throat. Kirsten drew her feet up and kicked him hard in the chest causing him to stumble backwards. She rolled to her feet and saw Control picking up the gun. Kirsten made a rush for her, driving her shoulder into the woman's stomach, knocking her over again.

She was picked up by the hair by the bodyguard and who then used his other hand to clench Kirsten's throat. It was exposed and he gripped hard choking her. She reached up inside her jacket's sleeve before drawing out a small knife and she drove it straight into the man's side. He grunted and she gasped before she took it out and drove it in again and again before the man eventually let go. She dropped to the ground, saw Control again with the gun and moved in behind the man as the woman shot. The vegetation was split by a bullet and Kirsten drove her knee up into the bodyguard's stomach.

He doubled over and she head locked him, driving him backwards, straight into Control. She tumbled backwards letting the gun go to the ground. Kirsten turned to run after Craig, but she heard Control call on the voice comms, advising the man in the car that the man coming out should be shot dead, and any woman following should also be eliminated.

Kirsten ran hard down the path and withdrew her weapon from inside her jacket. She'd have to be quick because Craig should nearly be down there. She saw him turning the last corner before he would reach the car park and she sprinted hard, shouting out his name. He stopped and turned to face her as she continued to sprint at full pelt.

'Kirsten' he said, 'What are you doing? You gave me the wrong stuff.'

Kirsten didn't stop but leapt at him, hitting him just below his rib cage and knocking him into the undergrowth behind. She heard the silenced gunfire as it snaked through the trees.

'Stay down' she said. 'Don't get up.' Kirsten rolled off and dove into the undergrowth. She burst forth from it and into the car park, seeing the driver still beside his car. He would've had difficulty seeing Craig from where she'd pushed him to, but Kirsten was on a clear line of sight, and she ducked down behind a car as a shot broke the windscreen.

The rest will be coming soon too, she thought. *I need to take this guy head on quickly*. As Kirsten put her head up above the car, another shot rang out and she ducked down again quickly. He obviously had her pegged and Kirsten knew she'd be pinned down unless something changed. She had to do something though, especially with the other two coming.

Kirsten went flat to the ground and looked under the car. She could just see one of the man's legs, and with the gun ahead of her, she lined up a difficult shot. When she fired, she heard a yell and then the man hit the ground. She dived back into the undergrowth, shouting for Craig. The other pair must be up and about, she thought.

'Follow me. We need a car.' With that, she ran back into the car park to see a small white family car driving in. There were two people in the front, a man behind the wheel, along with a young woman. They had that feel about them as if they were somewhere they shouldn't be, but Kirsten didn't care. It was a good enough vehicle. As the man went to park it, Kirsten ran in front of him, banging the bonnet.

'Get out' she yelled. 'Get out.'

'What are you doing?' cried the man and then found a gun pointing at his head. He opened the car door, hands up in the air. 'Don't shoot. Don't shoot. You can have it. You can have it.' Kirsten looked over, saw the bodyguard coming into the car park. She took her weapon and fired two shots over in his direction, causing him to run for cover.

'Get in the back of the car' she said to the man, and he opened the car door without asking anything further. 'Get in the back' she said to Craig, and he jumped in while Kirsten took the wheel. She leaned over pushing the girl back against her seat and told her to roll down the window. As she did so, Kirsten took the gun and fired a couple of shots over in the direction of Control and her bodyguard.

'That's to keep them tied up for a bit' she said. Kirsten hammered the accelerator, racing the car out of the car park, back up the single road they'd come down. Kirsten didn't spare the horses. As the car reached the junction of the main road, she pulled out in front of another car, causing it to blare its horn wildly.

'What the hell is this?' yelled the man in the back.

'Shut up and you won't get hurt,' said Kirsten. 'I'm taking your car, but I'll drop you further up here.'

'Who are you?' said the man.

'It doesn't matter. What matters is unlike those people I won't shoot you, not unless you give me cause to.' Kirsten saw a bus stop up ahead, quickly pulled the car over, and told the man and the woman to get out. 'Just go' she said. 'Just go.'

As Kirsten drove away, she saw the man taking his phone. He was probably calling the police but that was fine because she was going to ditch the car anyway. As she drove along, she saw a train station, one of the small ones, and she parked the car up beside it.

'Time to get out, Craig, let's go,' she said. She spun out into the back, taking her rucksack onto her back, demanding that he start to run.

'Is there a train coming?' asked Craig.

'Like heck there is,' said Kirsten. 'The last thing I'm doing is going on the train. Come on.'

She ran away from the train station before jumping over the

tracks further down, making off across fields. It took a half-hour of running before they reached a small village. Kirsten ran to the bus stop consulting a small, printed timetable on the shelter wall.

'Good,' she said. 'We're in luck. Five minutes and we've got another one coming. We'll be back in Aberdeen in no time.'

'Is that where you're basing yourselves at the moment?' asked Craig.

'You don't ask questions at the moment,' said Kirsten harshly. She saw the man's face fall. 'Listen,' she said, 'I was in that caravan at the amusement park. Somebody put a bullet in Anna Hunt.'

'Weren't you meant to be doing that? That's what Control said. Said I was to keep an eye on you, make sure nobody else interfered.'

'Well, you didn't do a good job of that,' said Kirsten. 'Feels to me like everybody's interfering.'

'They said Anna's got some colleagues, looking out for her, trying to help her escape.'

'Listen to yourself, Craig. Anna's got colleagues helping her escape. When did Anna Hunt ever need an escape plan? She's got her own one and then what? Her sister's in trouble? If she was really going to run like that, she would have got her sister out.'

'They said she's a traitor. She's got secrets she's passing on.'

'Have you got proof of that?' asked Kirsten.

'Of course, I don't. It's come from up the line, higher up. Control.'

'Control who just tried to shoot you? Control who was going to put a bullet in your back if I hadn't been there?' Kirsten watched the man's face. A sudden realisation that he didn't know whose side he was really on.

'Where are we going then?' asked Craig.

'We're going somewhere where we can lie low and work out what's going on here. There's the bus. Get on up the top. Sit at the back and I'll sit two rows in front of you.'

The bus was a double-decker. As Kirsten reached the top, she saw Craig at the back. She peeled the free paper off the seat in front and sat down with it, constantly looking over the top to see who was getting on the bus. The journey back to Aberdeen was quiet, just normal, everyday people making their travels back to the big city.

On arrival at the bus station, Kirsten took Craig by the hand and told him to act like they were a couple. She walked less than half a mile away before marching into a hotel and asking for a room. She signed the book as Mr and Mrs Smith, giving a wink to the man behind the counter. He simply smiled at her. She walked up the fitted carpet of the three-star hotel, making her way to the very top room that they had been assigned. Carefully, she used the key card to open the door, pushed it open, and invited Craig to walk inside.

Once he'd stepped inside, she followed him and closed the door. He went to turn around, but she pressed him up against the wall and began to frisk him. She took out a gun and threw it to one side and then found a knife down his leg as well.

'That's enough,' said Kirsten.

'What are you doing?' asked Craig. 'You know I'm glad to see you. You're all right, but what are you at?'

'You,' said Kirsten. 'You were there outside the caravan. I didn't ask you to meet me there, yet you came.'

'I told you, I was under orders. I was going to meet you afterwards,' said Craig.

'That would have been better. Instead, I find you with the same person that gave me orders. Orders that don't seem to marry up. I don't know if I can trust you at the moment, Craig.'

'Of course, you can. This may be business and that, but I'd never harm you.'

Kirsten wondered what to do. She took Craig from the wall and threw him face down on the bed with his hands up behind back restrained, and took off the tie he was wearing, tying it around his hands. She then picked him back up and hit him across the back of the head with the gun, causing him to black out and fall to the bed.

What do I do? Kirsten thought what her options would be. Then she placed a phone call into Dom. It took Dom about an hour to get there, but when he did, she led him into the room advising him she wanted to know if Craig was telling the truth. Dom looked at her.

'Haven't you asked him?'

'No. I've not touched him either.'

'What do you need me for?' asked Dom.

'You need to find out. Do it properly. Physically, if you need to. Use a bit of force. I can't do that.'

'Is he something to you?'

'He was,' said Kirsten. 'He might still be, but my judgment is flawed on this. I need an old hand like you, Dom. An old hand to tell me what I should think here.' She relayed to Dom all that had happened since dropping off her package at the train station.

'Okay,' he said. 'I'll get this done, but probably best you go for a walk. In fact, go and get me some water or something. Give me about half an hour.'

Kirsten left the room, went downstairs, and wandered

round Aberdeen, sticking to the backstreets where she found a supermarket that was open, picking up a couple of bottles of water and some food.

She walked around for a while before making her way back to the hotel room approximately half an hour later. As she entered, she heard a thwack. Dom, possibly hitting Craig with the back of his hand.

'Ah, so you've returned,' said Dom, and he made his way over to Kirsten taking her to one side. Over her shoulder, Kirsten could see the bruised face of Craig.

'I've done it properly,' said Dom. 'He's clean. I can't find any cause for suspicion. I think he's genuinely confused.'

'What is it, Kirsten?' Craig spat. 'What is it you want from me?'

'I want you to disappear,' said Kirsten. 'Dom says you're clean, in which case you got played.'

'I got played by you! Was this all a test?'

'Just at the moment, I don't know who to trust, and yes, this is a test, but you've come through.'

'You didn't have to do this,' said Craig. 'You could have trusted me. I'm here for you. You know that. Our time together should have told you that.'

'Look, Craig,' said Kirsten, 'I don't know who's coming for me. I don't know who's involved in what I'm doing at the moment. I was kind of hoping you might have some explanation, but it seems that Control took you in and nearly hung you out to dry as well. Just go and stay safe.'

'I could help you,' said Craig. 'Do your work in the field? I know what I'm doing.'

Kirsten shook her head.

'You're compromised,' said Dom. 'That's the problem.

People know you've been involved. Time to go, okay, and I'll see you around. Don't tell anyone anything or where you've been. In fact, if I was you, I'd go and hide until we know this is all done.'

Craig looked over at Kirsten, and she nodded. 'They tried to kill you today, Craig. They'll do it again and you may not see them coming. Go to ground until you hear it's safe.' Craig nodded, reached up and felt his bruised chin. Kirsten could see the bruising, all over the face, and down the side of his arm until he put his jacket on.

'For what it's worth, Craig', said Kirsten, 'I'm sorry.'

'Not as much as me,' he said. 'Not as much as me.'

Chapter 19

Dom took Kirsten back to Montrose in a taxi, dropping them off on the edge of town. They walked through several streets to a small caravan park where Dom showed Kirsten to a caravan at the rear of the site. Inside, she found the rest of the team and was handed a coffee from Carrie Anne almost as she walked in through the door.

'How did it go?' asked the concerned blonde-haired woman.

'Well, Craig's not working for anybody else, but he got played.'

'You know that for sure?' said Carrie Anne.

'I worked him over,' said Dom; 'made sure I knew for real. He's clean. Thought everything he was doing was for genuine reasons, but Control isn't genuine. Control's somebody after whatever Anna's got.'

'Is there any good news?' asked Kirsten. 'Because at the moment I could do with some. It appears I've just offended one of the best things in my life and I'm no further on with finding out who's trying to kill us all.'

'I've got something,' said Justin. 'It wasn't quite Godfrey. I managed to get in touch with one of his sergeants, so to speak. I've got a translation on the code you had. We've identified a geographical location. I'm not trusting anyone, so I didn't tell him what it was for. He thinks it's some old things I'm working on. In fact, he seemed completely unaware of what we were up to, but now that Control's dodgy, that seems to make sense.

'It does indeed,' said Carrie Anne. 'I don't think Godfrey knows what's going on at all with regards to Anna.'

'I think I'm going to have another chat with Anna,' said Kirsten. 'I need to know where this all came from. I know she wants to keep it a secret; she wants to protect whoever her source is, but it's beyond that now. Justin, brief Dom and Carrie Anne where the location is for this item,' said Kirsten, 'I'm going to chat with Anna.'

Carrie Anne pointed to the far end of the caravan and Kirsten walked a short corridor, turning into a room that barely accommodated the double-sized bed that Anna was lying in.

'How did it go?' asked Anna, before taking one look at Kirsten's face and simply nodding. 'Hopefully, you believe me more now. I don't think Control's working for us. Possibly, she's working for the other side.'

'Who is that other side?' asked Kirsten. 'I've had it, Anna. I know you want to protect your source, but I need to know what's going on. I'm being shot at. I'm asking people out there to put their lives on the line, and we don't even know what this is for. We don't even know who you're working for.'

'I'm working for the same people I've always worked for, the British public,' said Anna. 'I'm as loyal as they come. Too loyal. I shouldn't have taken this on board.'

'But what is this? You know you can trust me. I've seen Control for what she is. She gave me the kill order on you, but she's not to be trusted, which tells me that whatever you're doing is sitting on the right side of the fence. Tell me what it is.'

'I'm just meant to trust you like that?' said Anna.

'Frankly, yes. I've kept you here. I've kept you away from everybody. If your job is to get at the truth and the best of it,' said Kirsten, 'then you tell me because then you're doing exactly what I'm doing.'

Anna sat up in the bed and Kirsten could still see that there was a drip attached to her arm. The doctor must have visited again, but Kirsten did think she looked less peaky than she had done before.

'Okay,' said Anna. 'Keep this one to yourself though. I was operating on a hint I got from a Belarusian diplomat. She said that somebody on the British side was supplying intelligence to Russia. Now that's kind of a wild claim and not one I'd report just like that, but when it's made by a diplomat in that way, quietly, compromising her if it was wrong, it was worth looking at.

'She had information about items that were being dropped. I tailed one of the porters from the Russian embassy. He wasn't a porter; he was an agent. It took me three months following his drop routes. He was very subtle, always went about different ways, but I could see him pick things up. The diplomat said that when they dropped the package on the third Tuesday of the month, that was the contact with the British agent.

'For two months, there was just a coded message and I couldn't break it. But on the third, when I picked it up, it was the location, but I was also spotted. They tried to chase me there and then,' said Anna, 'but I disappeared through the back streets of London. No one knows I have it except those who saw me. Now, my face isn't completely unknown. When I went back to my flat, it was trashed. I went straight into hiding at that point, used my two safe houses to let you know where I was going, but I had to leave something that only you could find out. Justin knew about Linda. He also knew about Walter though he never thought what it really was, so I'd have to send you to see Linda. I hoped you would've got her safe as well.'

'That didn't exactly work out right,' said Kirsten. 'Unfortunately, Dom made a mistake, but we got her back in the end. She's safe enough.'

'Who's watching over her?' said Anna. 'You're not—you're here.'

'She's up on Lewis. I have friends there. She's okay. Trust me.' Kirsten could see the relief on Anna's face. 'The good news is, Anna, Justin's been able to get a decryption of those coordinates.'

'Then you need to go there and find what it is. Whatever it is, get it to Godfrey. This thing's too big and it's growing arms and legs. Once it's with Godfrey, it's registered. It's there. It's in. He'll know where to put it, who to put it in front of, and if it needs decryption at the highest level, he'll have it.'

'Why wouldn't they have just recovered the item once you'd stolen the address?'

'Because the carrier won't know where it is. The one who wrote out the coordinates won't be from there. It'll be scrambled in a system. You can't backtrack it. That's the whole point. The way they run that cover is that it's generated in a random fashion through a system. You have to be able to get access to that system. You have to know that coding; that goes all the way back. They're still coming after me, so they haven't simply gone and found it.'

'What're you saying? You're saying that those people who put the message out have no idea where the item is?'

'Correct. The only person who'll know where it would've been is the contact. He was meant to receive the coordinates. We have intelligence on how they run these systems. Godfrey has information he can use to break codes. Those in the embassy in Russia don't know that.'

'And what? They'll not just simply report it back, get whoever it is that does know it to go and get it?'

'That item's too precious for that. They've been entrusted with it. The last thing they need to do is tell anybody they've lost it, because they haven't. Until I recover it, until I go anywhere else with it, it's not lost. They go back and say they've lost it, they're dead. At least that's what I'm assuming. It was precious enough for them to come and try and kill me. It must be big.'

'So, that's why they're watching us? Trying to find out what we're doing, but they're watching us well. Didn't tell anybody we were going to Aberdeen. Didn't tell anybody about the Waltzer. And still, there were at least two parties there.'

'Yet you're not being watched that well. I take it your recent trip went okay.'

'Nobody picked up where I was and I was able to follow Craig all the way back to Control.'

'You're doing something right,' said Anna, 'but they know the general area to look for you. They're spotting you. They may be using cameras within the towns. You went in disguise last time, didn't you?'

'How did you know?'

'Just a guess,' said Anna. 'That's why they couldn't get you, couldn't get your facial recognition. Don't trust that you can go to this place without them turning up.'

'What if,' said Kirsten. 'What if we play a little decoy of our own?'

'How do you mean?' asked Anna, adjusting herself in the bed, pushing herself up higher with her fists, grimacing when the discomfort set in.

'If I put myself out there, put most of the team out there, make up a new location, somewhere to draw them all in while I send somebody else off on their own to pick up the item.'

'You call them out like that, they'll come with everything because this is their end game. They have to pick up this item from you, destroy it or send it back, whatever, or their masters will come for them.'

'If the item is as important as you say it is, well, maybe it's worth the risk.'

'Just be aware that once you do that, the game's not over. Whoever picks up the item will still need to get it to Godfrey, still has to get it out of our hands and into somebody else's. They'll know you'll not be able to open it up, whatever it is. The Belarusian informant told me that. She was able to tell me a lot about how they work things, but she was most insistent that this item was key.'

'Okay,' said Kirsten. 'That's what I'm going to do. We'll run a decoy. We'll make it out to be somewhere completely different. Let them come.'

'Who's going to go and get it?' said Anna. 'I might be fit enough if the doctor lets me.'

'No,' said Kirsten. 'I don't trust you enough yet. You told me a story. I've got no proof about it yet. We find this item, then we'll get it to Godfrey. I'll pass it on to the highest-ranking officer in these services that I know. Then it's up to him.'

'Good girl,' said Anna. 'It's hard not to trust, isn't it? Especially the people you've trusted before, but I haven't given you anything that can be corroborated. Till you get the item, you've got nothing, but understand that once you have that item, you become me, the new target that they will hunt.'

'They should get the item then,' said Kirsten. 'I need somebody who can hide. I need somebody who can operate on their own. There's only one choice, isn't there?'

Anna looked at her and nodded. 'Dom has to go for the item. He's your most experienced operator. He can't fight like you can in a crossfire. He's not as good; it's not his thing. Carrie Anne can fight, and Justin, well, keep him well out of it.'

Kirsten sat down on a small chair on the side of the room, barely able to keep her legs in a gap away from the bed.

'We'll send Carrie Anne out, and once she's out and gone and we make sure they see her go, then she loses them. We'll say she's picked it up, she's coming for me, going to hand it to me, and all that time we'll send Dom off to get the real item.'

'Goodness sake. You're thinking like a proper spy now. Cross this and cross that and make sure they don't have a clue what's going on.'

Kirsten sat with her hands on her lap, her head now bowed down. 'It's risky, this. Can't just come in though, can we? It's what I want to do, is just bring it all in.'

'Unless you can prove that Control is not who she says she is, you won't get within five metres of the building, or she'll have people on you. You can't just march into the headquarters down in London. That won't work. You need to get in front of Godfrey. You'll need to hold the item in front of him, so he knows what it is.'

Kirsten stood up. 'You'd better get well soon. If this all goes wrong, it's coming back on you again.'

'It's always on me,' said Anna. 'The moment I accepted that information from the Belarusian official, it was always on me. It's merely been handed down amongst my lieutenants, and you're doing damn well, but this will be dangerous. Be very cautious.' Kirsten nodded and went to leave the room, but Anna reached over with her good arm. 'Kirsten, I mean it. Be very careful.'

Chapter 20

Having sat down and worked on their plan, Kirsten sent Dom away in the middle of the night. He was to go to the correct location, find the item that needed to be recovered, and then contact her. Once he was clear, Kirsten and the rest of the team would set up a diversion and she chose an aquarium at North Queensferry. It was out of the way, miles from where Dom was on the west side of Scotland, closer towards Glasgow and up near Stirling.

Before she left, Kirsten went to see Anna Hunt again. She stared at the woman who simply kept looking out the window from behind the blinds that shielded her.

'Just make sure they don't see you leave,' said Anna. 'I'm not exactly fighting fit yet.'

'He'll be back soon enough.' She caught Anna's look. 'You don't believe that, do you?' said Kirsten.

'There's a lot of heat on this one. I'll be surprised if Dom gets away cleanly, never mind yourselves. You're running his cover. That means you've got to keep it going as long as possible. Besides, how are you going to convince them that you've got the item? It's so unlikely it's going to be buried in an aquarium.'

'I just sent Carrie Anne away, made sure she's going to pick up some tail. She'll stop off, pretend to go into a locker at a certain leisure centre. Once she does that, she'll go quickly and directly to North Queensferry and down to the aquarium. I'll be waiting there. They have no idea how good she is at this. Sure, she can handle a gun but they don't know her other talents. She'll look like somebody scared with a package she doesn't want and doesn't want to hang on to.'

'Being a woman, the men will think her vulnerable, struggling to handle the pressure. Playing all the stereotypes, aren't you?' said Anna.

'It's what you taught me.'

'It's good,' said Anna. The two women stared at each other for a moment, unsure what else to say. Anna coughed.

'Thank you for getting Linda out. She doesn't deserve any of this. You're lucky you don't have ties.'

'That's a little cold,' said Kirsten. 'I'm lucky that my brother's lost his mind and can't remember me. That's the truth of it. I don't see that as luck. I lost family. Lost them all.'

'No, you still see your family in Inverness. Macleod, that sergeant of his, the Ross fellow. They were family. That was a hard wrench. Lucky that Macleod gave you the push.'

'The push into this? Some days it doesn't seem that fortunate.'

Anna laughed and turned away. 'You'd better get going,' she said. 'Your plan's a good one. Make it work.'

'Yes, boss,' said Kirsten, took one last look and left the room. Kirsten would wait another hour for Carrie Anne to be well clear of the building before she and Justin walked along to the train station. Once there, Kirsten made sure that she got herself in front of as many cameras as possible, all the while trying to look as if she thought she had good cover. Her hair was up under a baseball cap, and she was wearing a leather jacket and the jeans that she favoured.

Justin travelled separately, keeping out of the cameras, and got off several stops before Edinburgh. There was a depot there from the electric company and he had work to do. Kirsten's plan was that he would abduct one of the workers, take the van, and have it wait outside the aquarium. Justin would then go and work on the electrics, be ready to switch them off. This would provide not only Kirsten's escape but also Carrie Anne's. Carrie Anne would pretend to find an item and bring it to the aquarium. There, she would hand it over to Kirsten. Hopefully, at that point, everyone would be so focused on them that Dom over in Stirling would be able to get clear.

Despite Anna approving the plan, Kirsten still thought it to be risky, especially the aftermath. What if they all didn't connect? What if it was only Dom? It'd be up to him to find Godfrey. Doing that without Justin would be hard but Justin had the context and his computer skills to be able to get in and find Godfrey's itinerary. Kirsten realised more and more that they were a team, that it'd be hard to sacrifice any of them.

Sacrifice. She said that word so easily in a way she'd never have said it on the murder team. When did she start treating people like pawns? In some ways, they were becoming friends, something Anna had warned against in the past. Kirsten found that cold side hard to portray, difficult to carry through. Macleod for all his doggedness had taught her compassion; care for those out there and the hammer blow to those who would cause the evil.

She continued by train from Edinburgh up to North Queensferry where she alighted at the platform, followed the sign down the steep hills to the aquarium at the bottom. North Queensferry was located beside the Forth Road Bridge and the view as she came down towards the aquarium was stunning. There were tight roads that bent this way and that, meaning the cars wouldn't have to simply climb the irrepressible hill but there were also places hard to find cover in.

There was the red car that came past two to three times today. The old man who seemed to walk quite quickly when he shouldn't be able to. The girl on the skateboard out at this time of day with no friends. They were all possible tails. Even though she didn't want to deviate from her route to establish that they were, she allowed herself a little inner smile. So far, so good.

Kirsten entered the aquarium, bought herself a ticket, and then went directly to the cafe. She sat there drinking a fizzy Coke and was surprised by the number of people who had bought tickets and came to the cafe as well. Surely, you would walk off around the exhibition but they were being clever, coordinated, waiting. There was no point grabbing her. For if they did, Carrie Anne would be still be out there. Same with Dom. That was the main concern—had they got a tail on Dom? But she couldn't do anything about that. A voice spoke into her ear.

'Electrics acquired and I am in position. Give the call.'

Kirsten reached up and scratched her ear and sat and drank for another couple of minutes before stepping into the lady's toilets. Once inside, she quickly tapped her earpiece. 'Going radio silent at this point. All understood? Carrie Anne, not here. There'll be one call, one call only.'

'Acknowledged. I have a view of the car park. I'll advise when Carrie Anne's in place.'

Kirsten sat down on the toilet seat lid and saw several other feet come in. She flushed, opened the door, and almost surprised a woman who gave a little bit of a jump before she wiped her face.

'You gave me a shock there, love.'

The accent wasn't Scottish, which didn't mean much, but it certainly wasn't put on. Maybe the woman was genuine. Maybe she was part of the observation team. Who knew? Kirsten didn't really care. It took another hour until Justin spoke to Kirsten's ear.

'Carrie Anne has entered the car park. She's coming now. Standing by.'

Kirsten stood up from her drink and joined the aquarium exhibition. There was a ground floor of small tanks, and she wandered along looking at the colourful fish within. She saw crabs, fish the size of a thumbnail and others bigger than her hand. After browsing around for a bit, she went down to the lower level which housed an enormous fish tank.

Within it was a circular walkway, one that moved on its own, and as she approached it, she saw some people on the return leg. There seemed to be an unusually large number of groups of four couples. Many you'd think would have kids of a younger age. After all, it was mainly kids that came to the aquarium, wasn't it? Again, she gave herself an inner smile.

They are here, she thought. Kirsten stepped onto the walkway and either side of her was a see-through concave behind which swam so many different fish. An array of silvers and blues, all gleaming from the lights that were placed inside this tank. She was able to look straight up above her and see fish pass across from one side to the other. The mobile path continued along on its own slow pace, weaving this way and that before turning around and coming back on itself around the other side of the enormous tank. She could see someone swimming inside, air tanks on his back, working away at some sort of repair. He was probably genuine because they would've had to have been very organised to get someone into that tank.

As Kirsten reached the starting point again of the circular walkway, she saw Carrie Anne approaching it, but instead of getting off, Kirsten remained on it and continued back on the circular path. She didn't look back, but instead, when she got to the far end, she stepped off, standing on the fixed path beside the mobile one.

She guessed it was there for people who wanted to stop and look around for a moment, or maybe for the staff, if they were looking at something particular. Then she looked back at Carrie Anne, and she saw her coming with an envelope. She held it up in front of her.

This would be good because everything was closed in. When the lights went, there would be chaos. She walked back along the fixed path and almost collided into Carrie Anne when she arrived. She handed over the envelope and Kirsten screamed in her ear, 'Juliet, lights!'

Her hand flew to her weapon and she moved into the bend so that neither those on the return or the approach side of the walkway could see her but the lights stayed on as a rather large fish appeared in front of her face, opening its mouth as if there was nothing better in the world to do. 'Lights,' said Kirsten again.

'What the hell's up with the lights?' said Carrie Anne. 'Juliet, where's the lights; kill the lights.' There came a muffled noise across her earpiece.

Heck, thought Kirsten, *Justin's been compromised.*

'Back to back,' said Kirsten. 'You take the return. I'll take the approach side.' The pair stood at the corner where the bend wasn't severe and allowed a couple of metres between them. Kirsten peered around the corner. She saw a weapon being pulled and tried to pick out who was actually an agent and who wasn't. The three people she saw were all carrying weapons.

Blast, she thought, *this isn't good*. She caught the look of the diver in the pool. *What would she do? How was she going to get out of this?* A shot rang out, hit the brick wall at the bottom of the tank, and bounced around narrowly missing her legs.

'That's too close for comfort,' she said to Carrie Anne. 'Let's keep them at bay.'

Kirsten moved out and fired a shot down around about knee height. She didn't want to shoot too high, lest she break the tank wall and the water started coming in.

'Kirsten, there's too many of them. I've got at least six to seven coming down here. Large weapons too. It's not just a handgun one of them's got. We're not getting out of this one. It's going to be up to Dom.'

'Just hold them. Hold them back for a moment. A couple of shots, just to pin them.'

Carrie Anne fired as instructed and Kirsten did the same on her side, before moving back in.

'You're surrounded. There's no way out. Throw the package out, then lie down on the floor.'

'We're going to put our guns on the walkway so they'll come round,' said Kirsten. 'Don't shoot.'

Carrie Anne looked at Kirsten. 'So, this is it. Set the guns down and then come out lying on the floor as the moving walkway takes us round?'

'Too easy,' she said. 'I want to give Dom as much time as possible. How strong do you think that plastic or whatever it is above us is?'

Carrie Anne looked at Kirsten. 'How strong is it? You're not going to.'

'You can swim, can't you? I'm sorry about your hair, but you can swim.'

Chapter 21

Dom sat on the bus, unsure of the people behind him. As it rolled into one of Glasgow's busiest stations, he got up and stepped lightly off the bus before looking for those behind him. Then Dom quickly turned and cut in behind several different buses that were approaching, looking for their stand, horns blaring. Somebody called him a pillock, but Dom kept on dancing in between, out and about before disappearing out onto the open road, a route pedestrians were not meant to take.

He cut back along a side alley and stood waiting. A man and a woman came round the corner, but Dom took the man with a punch to the chin as soon as he arrived. As he was sent backwards tumbling into the wall, Dom grabbed the woman, striking her with his other fist causing her to fall to the ground. He delivered two swift kicks, one into the gut of each of them before he turned and ran. They wouldn't be getting up before he was out of there.

For Dom, it would be the train up to Stirling and once there, he'd have to make his way to the flyover. That was the intended location for a drop to Kirsten. She had said there would probably be heat on him, said they would pick him up at some point, follow him, but her ploy was that he would be the decoy or at least that's what they would think. Instead, Dom was the one after the real item.

He slipped his way into the shopping centre and made his way out to a street on the far side of Glasgow city centre. Above him were high buildings with fascinating architecture, sculptures that many far below never cast their eyes up to. There were two train stations, and he made his way to the more northerly before looking for his platform for Stirling.

As he stepped onto the train, he stood beside the door and then bent down as if there was something wrong with his shoe. From the corner of the eye, he watched every one that entered the carriage. When he was satisfied, he sat down on the seat, a flip-down one that was between carriages. It was opposite the toilet and far from the most salubrious place on the train, but he could watch people from here and it was near the door if he needed to get away. He stuck his leg out, bouncing it up and down every now and again when someone approached, pretending it was gamy. So far so good. He had a bit of heat but yes, so far, it was okay.

The ticket inspector came through and Dom obliged, handing his ticket over before they reached the first stop. However, when they had cleared the city, a second inspector came through asking for his ticket. Dom obliged again, then asked the man what time the Inverness train would be from Stirling. The man looked at him, pulled out a timetable from his back pocket, looked through it, and then put it away again, telling Dom it would be at least another three hours before the train would be ready.

There was no exact time given and Dom had noted the engineering works north of Stirling up through Perth, meaning a delay had been shown on the board in the station at Glasgow. One thing he knew about the guys and the girls who worked on the trains, they knew their timetables, and they also knew what was happening with each train. There hadn't been a time when Dom had gone to one, asked about this platform, that platform, and where and when, and they simply answered as if it was second nature. Few of them ever went for the timetable, certainly up here in Scotland. Maybe in the middle of London or somewhere, it was so busy that you couldn't know everything but here, they were little computational geniuses, something he deeply appreciated.

The long and the short of it was he'd have to watch when he got off the train because that inspector was an enemy. He knew he was safe. They wouldn't interfere with him until he'd found his package but once he'd got it, he'd have to move and move quickly.

Dom stepped off the train in Stirling and looked back along the track. This was the first time he felt alone, far away from his team. They'd be running the decoy. How long could they last and would they get away? Would he end up having to go back to Anna to try and find the information he would need to locate Godfrey? It was much simpler when there was a terrorist organisation, an enemy to infiltrate.

When they were coming in the other way, life got tough because you didn't know who to trust, but he trusted Kirsten. She'd been open and made the right call for him to go dark as soon as she realised that they—not just Anna—were under threat.

Dom looked at his watch. It was past lunchtime, but he hadn't eaten. He wandered along to the small cafe at the station, sitting down and ordering a tuna sandwich and a cup of coffee.

Five minutes to feed himself, have a look around, and see who was his tail. Trying as hard as he could to focus, his mind drifted back to Kirsten and to Carrie Anne. Sometimes in this game, you got close to someone, but you always distanced yourself because you knew you could lose them tomorrow.

He thought that with Kirsten. She was friendly enough and he could rely on her. She was a decent boss, but he didn't have ties to her, but he saw Carrie Anne in a different way. *Maybe it was time to get out,* thought Dom. *Maybe it was time to call this all quits, but she wouldn't come with him, even if she felt the same way about him as he did about her. He hadn't asked, but whenever they worked together, it was good. There was a banter, a banter that was beyond what he had with other female agents. So what if she was ten years younger? He was sprightly enough, wasn't he? At least he was at the moment.*

In truth, he was worried for her, worried about this whole plan. He wasn't in disagreement with it because he didn't have a better one, but he knew it was dangerous and he worried for her sake. As an agent, you got used to losing people; it happened in the job, but he didn't want to lose Carrie Anne. He wondered how she was doing.

* * *

'Are you ready?' asked Kirsten.

'Ready as I'll ever be.'

'Good,' said Kirsten, 'and remember, if this all goes wrong, this sort of thing's going to bring everybody in. Give yourself up to the right people. We'll get sorted and if you get out, get to Dom.'

'If I get out,' said Carrie Anne, 'I'm going to sort Justin first.'

Kirsten nodded, took her weapon, and aimed it at the ceiling in front of her. She asked Carrie Anne to do the same behind her and they began to fire. The first shot caused a crack, the second developed the crack, but Kirsten kept firing. Eventually, she saw a large chunk break off and the water started to pour through. A fish landed at her feet slapping around but the water continued and the see-through structure cracked even further. More water poured through and Kirsten found it was up around her knees and running back down along the circular walkway on both sides.

'What the hell are you doing? Come out now,' shouted someone and more shots were fired.

'Don't, you idiot,' shouted someone else. 'You'll crack the glass.'

'It's cracked already.'

Kirsten fought the water that was pouring in. It pushed her back against the wall, but she tried not to come out on either the approach or the return side, instead keeping her cover at the bend.

'How long do we wait?' asked Carrie Anne.

'Until it's full,' said Kirsten.

'That's a long way back.'

'You said you could swim.'

Carrie Anne turned round, almost laughing. 'You are crazy.'

'Besides,' said Kirsten, 'if we can, we can get up through the gap, go up into the lake, swim up to the top there. That'll fox them.'

'You'll not get through with that water pouring down. You can't swim through that. It's gonna keep coming.' Kirsten could see the point. The water was pouring in hard, now coming up past her chest. 'You've got nowhere to leverage on,' said Carrie Anne. 'You can't swim through that. You'd have to be pushed and it wouldn't be easy. You need someone here pushing you up.'

Then it was like a revelation on Carrie Anne's face. 'Go get Dom,' she said.

'No,' said Kirsten, 'no.'

'Yes,' said Carrie Anne, 'You're the one to do that. You're the one. If he can get the stuff to you, you'll get it. There's a reason you're in charge. Anna said to me once, "She's a tenacious little squirt", said she chose you because when you get knocked down, you get back up. You'll get this done. Now, come on.'

Carrie Anne moved over towards Kirsten and put her arms around her waist. 'Up,' she said, 'before it floods completely.'

Kirsten took a large breath then allowed Carrie Anne to point her into the gap where the water was pouring through. The pressure was immense. Kirsten tried to make herself as sleek as possible, hands pointed ahead of her trying to break the water flow.

Carrie Anne pushed up and Kirsten found herself being forced in towards the clear plastic structure that had previously defended the circular track from the water. She felt Carrie Anne push her legs round, and Kirsten was shoved to one side but now, was on top of the structure instead of looking at it from underneath. Above her was the large tank of water with all the fish.

Kirsten looked down and simply got a thumbs up from Carrie Anne before the woman dove into the water and allowed herself to be taken around the corner getting washed back down the approach path. Kirsten swam upwards, going as quickly as she could, breathing out. She broke the surface of the water only barely, sucking in what air she could, and then dived back down. The last thing she wanted to do was to appear there, to be seen from the edge, so she swam under the water to the far side of the aquarium tank.

In reality, it was more than a tank. It was a large pool for it was open to the air at the top and when she broke the surface, she found herself on the other side of what was a seal tank. She climbed up onto metal rungs, ran across the dividing metal wall, and found herself at the rear of the cafe. Dripping wet, she ran round the edge and went up the aquarium's steep steps that led back up to the small town of North Queensferry.

As she sprinted out of the car park, she looked around for Justin, but she could see no electrical van. *Where on earth is he?* she thought, but she didn't wait. Instead, she sprinted down the first street before cutting into a house. She was sodden and she needed a car.

The house was a small bungalow. As she made her way around to the back, she could see a woman inside. *Needs must,* she thought though she felt for the woman who was there. Kirsten rapped the back door and when the woman opened it, she stepped forward, taking her off her feet, pushing her all the way back up against the wall. Kirsten's hand clamped over her mouth.

'Is anyone else here?' she asked. She wondered what the woman must have thought looking at this bedraggled stranger, but the woman shook her head. 'I'm not going to hurt you,' said Kirsten. 'I will tie you up and I'm going to borrow your car, but I'm not going to hurt you.'

The woman's eyes showed fear, unsure of Kirsten. Kirsten, with her hand over the woman's mouth led the woman through the house until she found the bedroom. Once inside, she located several belts, tied the woman's hands behind her and her feet together, and laid her out on the bed. She wrapped a gag across the woman's mouth before she opened up the cupboard and started to undress, looking inside for something she could wear.

The woman was taller than Kirsten but of a much slimmer figure and Kirsten found that the woman's jogging clothes were about the most comfortable thing she could get on. Her leather jacket was sodden, but Kirsten shook it and took it with her anyway as well as a large coat belonging to the woman.

Once again, she knelt before her, 'I'm sorry I have to do this, but you won't be here for that long. I'll let the police know. Once I'm done at the other end, they'll come and get you. It'll be teatime at the latest. Here.' Kirsten fetched a glass of water from beside the bed and gave the woman a drink. 'Do you need the toilet?' she asked, and the woman looked at her, shaking her head. 'You best go,' said Kirsten. 'Tea time's a long way off.'

She helped the woman through to complete her ablutions before bringing her back and laying her on the bed again. 'Thank you,' said Kirsten. With that, she went into the kitchen, and spied the car keys hanging on a rack on the wall. She went outside and found the Renault Clio, fired it up, and drove it out of North Queensferry.

The baseball cap she'd had on was gone. Instead, she had a head scarf around her, with some dark shades. Kirsten applied heavy red lipstick on her lips. Her hair was still wet though she'd dried it as best she could, and she was chilled from having been in the tank.

She tried to focus. Dom. She needed to get to Dom, but all she could think about was Carrie Anne and the sacrifice she'd made. Was the woman okay? There was no time to think about that.

Chapter 22

Dom was worried. He'd retrieved the item from the coordinates easily enough and found a data stick within a metal canister. Carefully, he had put the canister back, pocketing the data stick, and then returfing the ground to make it look like no one had been there. However, when he had stepped away, he had heard something like a twig breaking. He was in a small wood outside of Stirling and, being the experienced professional that he was, he didn't react to the sound but simply stood up and began walking along the path.

The area had a graveyard at the far end. While Dominic walked along the path between the trees, he spied a chance and took a left into the graveyard, passing through a narrow gate. The gate was permanently open, made of wrought iron and, although it was meant to be black, it had rusted greatly. At the bottom of it, vegetation had grown up almost to a height of two feet and so the gate wouldn't move. Dom found himself having to squeeze in between the small gap and into the graveyard.

Before he made that manoeuvre, he checked behind him, making sure that no one was too close. Having seen the path was clear, he made his move and then ducked in behind a large gravestone. It took only a few moments before a woman, around six feet tall, made her way through the gate. Although she was tall, her frame was still ample enough that it was difficult to squeeze through. Dom watched her put one hand up and then drag the rest of her body. It was at this point that he chose to strike.

Stepping out from behind the gravestone, Dom put one hand on her shoulder, and the woman turned to flee but was trapped between the two parts of the gate. Dom withdrew a gun, put it to her head, and told her to come through quietly. As soon as she was clear of the gate, he told her to go to her knees, and then to crawl forward on them, a manoeuvre made harder by the long, split skirt she was wearing. Dom couldn't tell if the woman was frightened as her complexion was so pale any loss of colour wouldn't be noticed, but as he placed her head on the gravestone, with the gun sitting on top of it, he asked her quite simply, 'Who are you working for?'

'We have to bring you in,' was the simple reply. Dom thought of Craig, the London Man, caught up in a chain of events where he was only following orders. He thought the woman was probably the same, and so he put a hand into her coat pocket, and found some plastic bindings. He told her to put her hands behind her back, and he snapped the binding around her wrists.

'Are you on your own?' he asked.

She nodded.

'That's the incorrect response,' he said. 'You've given me no reason to not just dispatch you now.'

'One of our own, they said. They said you were one of our own, just following orders. I was going to take you in quietly. I wasn't looking to kill you.'

'Who are you working for?'

'Control, who else?'

'Who did you report to before Control?'

'Anna Hunt.' Dom let the woman rise up on her knees and helped her turn and put her backside on one of the gravestones.

'You were one of Anna Hunt's? When did they tell you she was . . .'

'A traitor? Communique came through to our boss. I didn't know who had sent it, but the boss said it was high up. Then we were routed to Control. The boss took his orders from her. It was all cleared through though, because he would have questioned it. We were simply to round you up. They showed us photographs of Benbecula, of Aberdeen, the mess your team has been making, along with Anna.'

Dom sat some distance away, his gun in his hand but no longer pointing at the woman.

'How long have you been in the game?' he asked.

'Two years,' she said. 'Guess this will be a quick exit.'

'I don't intend to kill you,' said Dom, 'I don't intend to kill anyone unless they force me to. Our boss got a kill order on Anna Hunt. We were told to find her and put her down, simply told she was a traitor. The boss followed those orders up until the point she had to kill her. You see, we've worked with Anna too long. She's got too high a standing. We require some evidence.'

'So did our boss, and he received a letter from Godfrey. Apparently, the man's high up. He knew him by name because of some dealings he'd had with him before. Of course, you don't just simply contact him, but Control brought evidence.'

'In a matter such as this,' said Dom, 'I think you would have wanted to speak to the man, not simply get some signed piece of paper.' The woman shook her head.

'He seemed quite happy with it, the boss.'

'Where's your phone?' The woman pointed to her pocket. Dom took it out, put it on the ground, and proceeded to smash it with his foot. When he saw the screen go dead, he handed the mess back to her, placing it beside her on the gravestone.

'I'm sure they'll supply you another. Sorry about that, but if you don't move, they'll trace it. They'll come soon enough now as well. You'll be okay, a little bit red-faced at having been caught. But listen, Anna Hunt's no traitor. We've met her, spoken with her. They're after something she's got.'

'Something you're getting for her,' said the woman, 'and you've got it. I was about to relieve you of it.'

'Well, I'm sorry to disappoint,' said Dom, standing up, 'but I'm much too long in the tooth to be caught out that way. How many have they got looking for me? Five, six?'

'I make it at least fifteen,' said the woman, 'and that's the ones I know about. I've seen other people as well.'

Dom glanced over. 'Others? Not from our side?'

'Not from any side I know. Probably the Russians trying to help her out.'

Dom shook his head. 'That'll be the Russians panicking, trying to get back the information that Anna's got. Do me a favour, don't trust Control. If she gives you any further orders, by all means, follow them, but don't trust her.'

Dom turned to walk away, and he heard the woman spit after him. 'Why should I trust you?'

'Because you're alive,' said Dom. 'If I was trying to get away with British intelligence, feed it back to my boss, you'd be lying there as dead as the man in that grave. I'm one of the good guys. Don't forget that.'

'You're going to a meeting with Stewart then,' said the

woman.

Dom turned. 'Why do you say Stewart? Precisely Stewart.'

'Well, we got your other one, Carrie Anne. That's her name, isn't it? Part of your team.' Dom could sense the woman trying to wind him up, and the concern inside for Carrie Anne was large. There was one bright side. The Russians hadn't got her; instead, it was one of their people. There was a chance yet if Control didn't get to her.

'Well, I'll have to wait and see who I give this to,' said Dom. 'Might just make a run for myself.' As he walked away, Dom was glad Kirsten had got clear. He was also glad that Justin Chivers had clearly not been caught either, but his heart felt for Carrie Anne. When you grew this close to someone, it wasn't easy.

Dom continued away from the graveyard and around the outskirts of Stirling, He stuck to streets that had no particular significance, picked up an old hat from a charity shop, slapped it over the top of his face, and walked along with a limp, like an old man. When he got to a housing estate, he cut through the back of it and across a farmyard until he arrived at the service station beside the A9. He took out a one-time pay-as-you-go card, sticking the SIM inside his phone and then texting a message to Kirsten. She'd reply on a similar device before the two of them would break the sims. His message was simple. 'At Services. Two hours.'

Dom looked around and realised that night was falling. Beside him, there was a thin layer of snow on the ground, and he was glad they were in the lowlands. Any further north, and he'd be marching through the stuff, probably ankle-deep, at least. At the services, he saw a small hotel, basic pay for the room type. He stepped inside and made his way to the toilets.

Once there, he locked himself away inside a cubicle before taking off his hat, reversing his coat and preparing himself for the exchange. Kirsten would be in a car and he'd get a signal when she'd arrived.

It took another two hours before he heard the beep come through on the SIM card and he knew she'd be in the car park outside. Dom stretched his legs. He'd been sitting, cramped up, on the toilet lid. The hotel was quiet and certainly the reception toilets were extremely quiet. The bar had not been opened yet, but it soon would be, and his hiding hole would become a busier place.

Dom exited the building, stepped out into the car park and began walking around. He could see the CCTV camera, knowing he'd probably be picked up at some point.

Cars were moving in and out now at quite a rate. He saw one at the far end with a woman in the front. She was small, her brunette hair falling out behind her. She turned and Dom saw a pair of glasses, but it was clear who it was. The woman reached forward to the tip of her nose and pushed the glasses back up. It was an old habit from when she had them in the police force, something she was well known for when she wore glasses. It was a trait she'd found hard to break. The glasses she was wearing would be false ones, but Dom knew it was Kirsten.

The car swung around in the car park, and drove up towards Dom. Two cars in front stopped suddenly. One seemed to be waiting for a parking place, but in the one behind, Dom could see at least four adults. His senses pricked up. *That couldn't be right? That seems an awful lot.*

The car at the front had two men in it, both wearing suits. Dom turned away and made his way towards the other side of the car park. Out of the car stepped two large men. Dom could see the guns at their sides. They weren't in suits, but in jeans and jackets.

As Dom saw one reach for a weapon, he dived in amongst the cars parked within the spaces beside him. The windscreen of the car above him exploded. Dom crawled quickly behind more cars, then realised there was more gunfire. A cry hit the air, but Dom kept down low sprinting in between the cars, making his way down to the exit road from the services. Hopefully, Kirsten had put the car into reverse. When he got four cars along, he looked up, but he couldn't see her car. The bright side was, she wasn't trapped, she'd obviously been able to get out. The downside was she hadn't taken him with her.

Dom reached the exit road where a couple of cars were parked in terror and one began to try and drive off. Dom skirted around it, and gunfire came across his position. He got low behind the car, heard the glass in it again shatter before a tyre blew out. Quickly, Dom leapt into the trees beside the road. It was about five hundred metres from the car park down to the flyover over the A9. Dom reckoned if he could get there, he might be able to hijack a car, drive off, get to somewhere and hide out again. The key thing he had to do was to keep running.

As he reached the petrol station, he felt his phone ringing and he picked it up to see a text message. *Under the flyover*, it said, quite simply *under the flyover*. Dom ran into the petrol station forecourt but saw a car door open and a man step out with a gun. He fled to the other side of the petrol station, hoping he wouldn't fire. He knew there were two groups here because there'd been a firefight. The British side would never have pulled a gun like that, but if the Russians were after them as well, they clearly weren't bothered. That's if they were Russians at all and not simply mercenaries.

Dom ran round behind a car that was trying rapidly to get away, then cut back in behind the petrol station. He thought that if he didn't see Russians, he wouldn't fire, keen not to shoot his own side even if they were hunting him. As he made it to the flyover with the large roundabout above the A9 dual carriageway below, he saw a car grinding to a halt. A number of cars pulled to one side and then spread themselves across the road, causing everything to slow down. Dom ran past them, and he heard the cry of, 'Stop!'

He ran on, reaching the flyover where he gripped onto the rail, looking down the road below him. The traffic was racing past. He hoped Kirsten would be there.

'Don't move. Put your hands where I can see them,' said a voice behind him. Dom put his hand in his pocket, and grabbed the data stick, and then slowly began to raise his hands, making sure he had the data stick covered over by his fingers. He turned around slowly and could see two men and a woman looking at him.

'We're here to take you in,' they said. 'Let's do this slowly, carefully.'

'I'm not here to hurt anybody else,' said Dom, 'but you do know we're not the only two parties here.'

'We know. They've gone. It's just you and us now. Let's do this quietly. Nobody else has to suffer,' said the man persuasively. Dom looked at him. The man must have been in his early thirties. Beside him was a younger man, both looking fit as a fiddle, alongside a woman with a face that looked like she could wrestle with sledgehammers.

'Some of the agency's best I see,' said Dom. 'Well, you got

me,' he said.

'Just keep your hands where they are.'

'Where is it?' asked the woman. She had short-cropped black hair and was approaching him. Equal to his height, Dom thought she looked like she could throttle him with just one hand. He swallowed as she approached. He saw her put her hand inside his coat, patting down both sides. Then she looked up at his hand.

'Give me the contents of your left hand to me,' she said. Dom opened the hand slowly. There was nothing inside. The woman looked across to his other hand, and Dom opened it slowly, again revealing nothing.

'Where's the damn stick? Where's the thing you killed for?' said the woman.

Dom slowly turned around and looked down at the motorway below. He'd been positioned just above the hard shoulder. The different coloured asphalt ran from one side to the other, up and down in an area approximately three metres long.

'It's funny,' said Dom, 'I could've sworn I dropped it down there.' He felt his arms being taken behind him, restraints being put on him.

'You'll tell us where it is,' said the woman.

Dom shook his head. 'How do I know? It's a long way from here by now.'

Heading back towards Glasgow, less than half a mile away in a small car was Kirsten Stewart. She was smiling because on the seat beside her lay a small data stick. Carrie Anne had been captured. Dom, too. Justin was missing. She had to get this to Godfrey, or all of it would be worth nothing at all.

Chapter 23

The hour had just turned midnight and Kirsten was sitting in her second car of the day. The first one she'd stolen from a woman in North Queensferry. The second, she'd taken from a car park just outside services near Glasgow. She'd also swapped the number plates with a car she'd seen apparently abandoned in the far corner of the car park. It had a flat tyre, and enough rust on it to make her think it had spent years going through the sea and not the roads of the southern half of Glasgow.

Kirsten knew she had to make a move, but how and where? Godfrey was the key, but she had the data stick. She had to get it to Godfrey. Anna said he'd be able to translate it, whatever encryption was on it, Godfrey would break it or know someone who could. Godfrey would also take her seriously because he took Anna seriously. The two of them had gone far back in the annals of the services and Anna had been emphatic that Godfrey would be the solution to all of this.

Kirsten's team were down, Carrie-Anne and Dom both captured, and she hoped to God it was by her own side. There were clearly other influences at play, influences that wouldn't hesitate to kill, but now, those ideas were driven to the back of Kirsten's mind.

She had hoped to contact Justin Chivers, but she'd heard nothing, nothing at all. She tried going to the SIM card number she had for him but again, nothing. She sat with the car headlights out in the dark corner of the car park occasionally munching on a small sandwich she had purchased. She'd gone in wearing her headscarf, doing her best to keep clear of any CCTV cameras, but in truth, she knew with nowhere to go, she'd come undone. *Where was Godfrey?* she thought. *How do I get hold of him?*

She didn't know the man's other name. If indeed, this was his name. Maybe it was his code. He was delightfully English when she'd spoken to him, an older man with eloquent speech but he also carried with him a gravitas that give Kirsten an instant respect for him. Surely, he would listen to her. After all, she had stopped that train. She prevented the cruise ship from being blown to pieces. Yes, it was damaged, but they managed to save most of the people. Certainly, no one had gone overboard that hadn't deserved it.

She tried Justin Chivers once more but again, there was no reply. Time was moving on, so Kirsten decided she would have to bite the bullet and contact the only other person left she could trust in this situation. It wasn't her former boss Macleod because this would have been too far out of his comfort zone. He'd have been too formal in what he would do. She didn't want to involve Hope or any of the rest of the team either. She'd have to go direct to the one person who worked in this business who she knew currently, but who probably didn't want to know her.

She picked up her phone and dialled the number for Craig,

her London Man, who she had pressured so recently in Aberdeen. The man she had let Dom extract information out of, only to find that he was clean and was operating from the best of intentions when he'd come to see her.

She pressed the dial button and listened to it ringing. She was operating on a Pay-As-You-Go SIM, one she'd given to Craig, along with one to herself so they could communicate off the grid. The agency didn't need to hear what they were going to be saying to each other. They had to have the occasional secret, but she never intended it to be like this. Kirsten swallowed hard listening to the ring of the phone. It rang at least eight times. When she was about to hang up, she heard a click at the other end. There followed silence.

'It is me,' said Kirsten.

'Not so easy to speak with the bruised jaw,' said Craig.

'Sorry,' said Kirsten, 'I didn't know. You were in the wrong place at the wrong time. Anna was being shot.'

'You didn't really know me at all. That's what you want to say. That's what you need to say. Don't tell me you were just doing your job, just staying safe. I need to know you can trust even through all of this. You need to be able to trust someone,' said Craig.

'You were right there when they shot Anna. Right there when the windows blew out to the caravan, when I was scrabbling about on the floor for my life. Then you were gone. You weren't my knight in shining armour, standing, defending me.'

'With all due respect,' said Craig, 'I didn't know who the hell was shooting at who. I had been sent there, sent there to meet you. To bring you in, to talk about how it was going. They told me you had a kill order on Anna Hunt and I felt uncomfortable, and I could see her in the caravan. I could see you in there too, and she wasn't dead,' said Craig. 'Do you know what I thought?'

'You thought I was in league with her.'

'No. I thought you were being you, looking to see if it was for real. You wouldn't kill someone unless you had a damn good reason, and I hadn't been told any reason. I figured you probably hadn't either, so you were going to take your time. You were going to find out from Anna what was happening. Then somebody started shooting up the world.'

'I'm sorry for what Dom did to you. I couldn't do that myself.'

'Well, I guess that's something. They're still looking for you. You know that, don't you?'

'And if you tell them, they can probably trace this phone,' said Kirsten.

'I won't tell them,' said Craig. 'I don't know what you are to me but you're not just an agent. You're not just some bit of work.'

The phone went silent. Kirsten could feel her legs trembling almost like she was giddy, back to her school days. She hadn't realised how much he had meant to her until she had to go against him, had to question everything about him. He'd crawled in under her skin and she'd never seen it coming, and now here she was looking for more from him after practically throwing him to the wolves.

'We're not out of the woods yet,' said Kirsten.

'Out of the woods?' said Craig. 'You're right smack in all of it.'

'I need your help.' Again, there was silence on the phone. 'It's not a ploy. I'm not trying to find out about you,' said Kirsten. 'This is it. This is the end game. If I can make this work, we might just get away with it. Get away without any more death, without anybody else being put down.'

'What do you need?' asked Craig.

It was very matter of fact, but Kirsten almost wept at the sound. 'We need to find Godfrey, the man you took me to when you first met me.'

'Why?'

'Because Anna says he's the one who can help. I have information that he can use.'

'You realise who Godfrey is, don't you?' said Craig. 'High up, not high up in the public perception, but high up. One of the highest you'll never meet, and I've got you suspected of working with a traitor, suspected of letting her live while she hands over her state secrets.'

'You know that isn't true, don't you?' said Kirsten.

'What I know is very little. I know I was sent to make sure you were doing your job and you weren't. I know that you set me up and had one of your group beat me up to find out if I was genuine in what I was doing. I know you're hiding from everyone. I know that your team has just been busted and everyone is combing the ground looking for you, and I know I'm putting my neck on the line simply by speaking to you.'

'But do you think I'm right? Do you think I've got at least a shot in the dark with this?'

'What makes you think that?' asked Craig scornfully.

'You never gave them our SIM card. You'd have known I was at my end of my tether; you'd have known there were very few places I could go and I've come to you, but you never offered that up to them. You could be a hero and bring me in.'

'True,' said Craig. 'Very true, and don't get me wrong; there's a part of me would love to for the humiliation and pain you made me suffer at that man's hands, just to believe me when my words wouldn't do. Who I am to you didn't do! Oh, don't think I didn't think about it. Don't for one minute imagine it didn't cross my mind.'

'She didn't do it,' said Kirsten. 'And you didn't betray me, even though I put no trust in you.'

'I'll tell you where Godfrey is because he landed in Scotland today. There's a small castle on the way up the A9, Grey Abbotts. It's not far from Blair Atholl, but it's not one of the ones that all the public go to. Much older, privately owned, hidden away in the back.'

'I know of it,' said Kirsten.

'Good,' said Craig, 'because that's where he is tonight, and he'll be there probably up late discussing a lot of things.'

'How do you know this?' said Kirsten. 'I thought you'd have to go and dig up sources. He keeps his movements very quiet.'

'Not when you drive him there. I'm not there of course now. I'm sitting down in the village. If you want, I'll give you a hand.'

Kirsten swallowed hard. After all she'd put him through, he was still offering to help, and yet inside her a voice was saying, *Is this his thing? Is he going to bring you in? Is this a trap to get you to come to him so he can grab you and take you in?*

'You're wondering again, aren't you?' said Craig. 'That's why you'll be good at this job. That's why they won't catch you out often because you're a suspicious bugger, like Anna Hunt, question everything. You'll need to learn when to leave that at the door,' said Craig. 'Otherwise, like Anna Hunt, you'll be alone.'

Kirsten could feel a tear welling up and rolling down her cheek. 'Don't come with me. Stay where you are.'

'Because you don't trust me?'

'No,' said Kirsten, 'because if this goes wrong, they'll put you away, they'll put me away, they might even put us six feet in the ground and I can't have that for you. I work best alone, anyway,' she said.

'Just be aware,' said Craig, 'it's Godfrey; security around him will be tight. It will be our people as well. You don't want to kill off a load of them and then present Godfrey with a prize. It's not going to work like that.'

'Then we'll have to do it the quiet way,' she said. 'Craig, please stay out of it. Please stay away. I don't want your help.'

'What is it that you want?'

'Your forgiveness,' she said, and hung up. Kirsten took the SIM card out of the phone, snapped it, rolled down the window, and threw it out onto the asphalt of the car park. She slammed her hand against the wheel of the car over and over again. She couldn't lose him; she couldn't.

Kirsten pulled her seatbelt across, turned on the lights of the car, started it, and began the drive up the A9. Blair Atholl was probably a good two hours away, situated up beyond Perth. If she kept good time, she could be there in the early hours of the morning. Godfrey might be asleep or he might be up in negotiations, but it would be dark and she could maybe make her way in. But Craig was right; the people guarding Godfrey would be her own, her own side. There wouldn't be Russians there. There wouldn't be the crossfire hell she'd known before, people shooting and she not knowing who they were from. These people would be her own. She'd have to do this without hurting others in the process.

Chapter 24

Once she had reached the turnoff that lay beyond Blair Atholl, Kirsten drove up into the mountains. The estate lay on the far side, and she'd only come past this way once before. In the dark, it was hard to make out what was going on, but she could see the car sitting at the side of the road approximately half a mile from the estate. She'd need to go in on foot.

Having risen up the mountain, the snow now lay thick around her. Kirsten pulled off the road well before she reached the protective car. There was a short track down to a farmhouse and she could see no lights that were on. Kirsten, with her own lights killed, stopped the car, and got out, quickly racing to the rear of the farmhouse. The noise of the car had obviously woken someone, and she heard a dog bark briefly before being quietened. The rear door of the house opened, and a man stepped out, looking around before he made his way over towards her car. The dog hadn't followed him, and Kirsten snuck up quietly before clamping a hand over his mouth, kicking him in the back of the knees and driving him to the ground but holding him tight.

'I don't want to hurt you, sir, and I certainly don't want

to hurt anyone else in your house. Is there anyone else in there?' The man shook his head. Kirsten moved her arm tighter around the man's throat. 'Is there anyone else in there, sir?'

The man started to choke slightly and then nodded.

'I'm going to take my hand off your mouth briefly. You're going to tell me who, and you're going to say it quietly. If you shout out, I'll twist your neck and snap it.'

Kirsten had no intentions of doing this, but when she took her hand off the man's mouth, he quietly told her that the grandkids were upstairs.

'Good,' said Kirsten. 'Where's the dog?'

'He's in the kitchen,' said the man.

'Is the kitchen door closed?' The man nodded. 'Is there any way for the dog to get out?' The man shook his head. 'Just confirm that to me,' said Kirsten, 'and be advised that if the dog can get out of that kitchen, I will shoot it. You will have a dead dog. Tell me again, is there any way for the dog to get out?' The man shook his head.

'He's closed in,' he said. 'Trust me, he's closed in. I'm not going to risk my grandkids.'

'Neither am I,' said Kirsten. 'We're going to walk back in. I'm going to tie you to a chair in the living room. You probably will be able to get out of it, but it'll take you some time. What you won't do is tell them about my journey south because if I hear you've had contact with the police or anyone else, I'll come back to this house. So, let's go in and I can brief you further.'

Kirsten let the man stand up but kept his arm bent up behind his back. He made his way in, and she took him through to a living room at the front where the embers of a fire were dying.

'Sit in the chair, please,' said Kirsten.

The man looked at her pitifully. 'Please don't,' he said. 'They're my grandkids. Don't. They can't see this.'

'And they won't see anything,' said Kirsten. 'You just happen to be the unlucky person on the way. You some sort of a farmer?'

'We have some land further down towards the valley. There are some fields down there as well. We don't grow much. We've been trying. I have a small selection of greenhouses.'

'Do you have fertilizer?' The man nodded. 'Where is it?' asked Kirsten.

'Shed out the back.'

'Any red diesel? Anything else that ignites?'

'There's everything in there. It's all in that shed. Have a look. Take what you need,' said the man, 'just don't hurt my grandkids and don't leave me as a mess for them.' Kirsten walked over to the man who was now sitting down and she reached for a tie that was sitting on the chair.

'Smart one this,' she said. 'You wearing it earlier?' The man nodded. She took one wrist and tied it tight. She did the knot at least three times.

'You will sit here until five. If at that point you wish, you may untie this knot. Oh, don't worry. It's quite easy to undo. Then you can go to your grandkids. If I come back into this house before then and that knot is untied, I will shoot you and I will leave the mess you don't want your grandkids to find. Up until then, you can do what you want in that chair with your book, magazine. I'll even put the TV on for you if you want.'

The man stared incredulously at Kirsten, 'But you don't hurt my grandkids,' he said.

'Trust me. I don't want to,' said Kirsten. 'Now I'm going. Be good.' The man nodded profusely.

Kirsten made her way out to the barn at the rear of the house and found it unlocked. Stepping inside, she saw an array of fertiliser, paraffin, red diesel, some petrol, and a number of powders which gave her an idea. She looked around for a bottle and over the next twenty minutes, mixed a concoction that would make a surprisingly loud bang.

She found a rucksack nearby, placed her concoction within that rucksack, threw it over her shoulder and went to step out into the snow. As she did so, she saw the coverall hanging by the door. The man had clearly been painting and the white coverall had the occasional fleck across it, but it was mostly white. She put it on, wrapping it up around the clothing she was wearing. It would be good in the snow. Then she pulled the hood up round her head. She probably had at least a fifteen-to-twenty-minute walk now to the perimeter of the estate she was about to infiltrate.

The night was cold, bitterly so. Kirsten could feel the chill in her bones, but she threw that to the back of her mind as she walked across the mountainside, stepping through the white powder, glad she still had her boots. As she got closer, she tried to keep more of the mountainside between her and the estate edge before going down on her belly and crawling the last five hundred yards. She couldn't see any cameras, but there would be some about and as she reached the fence she took the backpack off, leaving the concoction she'd prepared before.

The man had also had the right materials to mix up a long fuse and she tailed it away behind her over some one hundred metres. It had been a hard carry in the rucksack, but she'd managed it and now, here at the end, she put her arm around the little blowtorch she had found in the shed. Cautiously, she hit the clicker. It ignited. Kirsten almost scorched her hand, trying to keep the flame hidden as she lit the long fuse she had poured out.

She watched it burn slowly before she began to run as hard as she could across the snow, around to the other side of the estate. High above her stood what Craig had described as the castle. In truth, it wasn't that impressive and, in fact, only one part of it was a castle, a long towering spire with the rest of it a modern building constructed around it.

Kirsten ran hard, her breath feeling cold inside her as she sucked in lungfuls of air. As she got what she thought was a good distance away, a loud explosion roared into the night with a brilliant amount of flame showing down by the fence where she'd left her explosive device. She saw lights go on, people making their way out towards the fence, confusion reigning.

Kirsten was now at the far end of the estate where she climbed up the fence and pulled herself over the top. Her coverall suit got caught on the barbed wire, but she extricated herself from it as she then tumbled down into the white snow beyond. She was back to her sportswear that she had originally taken from the woman in North Queensferry. She felt her arms were exposed, but she ran as hard as she could toward the edge of the castle.

Looking around for an entrance in the side, Kirsten couldn't see any until her foot hit something metal. She tapped down hard twice, all the time listening to the cries at the far end and the dogs that were beginning to be let loose. Kirsten dug away the snow beneath her and saw a small round metal lid. It was about the diameter of herself, and she reached down and pulled at it, but it was heavy.

Using her fingertips, she was able to pry it up and gently, she moved the lid across. The smell that came out was almost unbearable. Kirsten didn't care, allowing herself to drop down into the sewer below. She reached up, dragged across the lid of the sewer as best she could, and fixed it shut.

Looking down to see which way the excrement was flowing, Kirsten splashed her way along the sewer. She made sure to go upstream. The building up above may have been newer, but it fell into pipes that were old, and which probably joined up to newer works further down.

She was improvising. This she knew, but really, she had little other choice. The sewer ran along for about one hundred yards before it split, both sides getting smaller. She followed the one to the left first until it ended up in a pipe, but there was no way she could get up through. Kirsten doubled back, took the right-hand route, and found herself coming up against a metal grid.

There was a concrete floor on the side of it and no lights showing. There was no wind here, so clearly, she would be inside, but quite where, she wasn't sure. She reached up and felt the metal grid move and was able to push it forward, allowing herself to climb out into a concrete room. There was one door out of the room and Kirsten replaced the grid slowly before making her way over to it.

Kirsten stank. Of that one thing she was now sure. There would be no time to clean herself down, no time to get rid of the smell. She'd have to move quick and find Godfrey. She touched the top of her chest where the crop top she was wearing had a funny shape to it. The data stick was secure. Then Kirsten moved closer to the door that led out of the concrete room.

Here was where they clearly dumped any of the excess rubbish, any of the excess muck of the house. Was she about to move into the rear of the stables? She turned the handle of the door slowly and found that it gave way. She pulled the door back, and a spot of light fell into the room.

There was no squeak from the door and for that, Kirsten was glad, for ahead of her with his back turned was a man. Kirsten moved quickly, hitting him in the back of the neck and then again towards the head, knocking him to the ground and out before he had a chance to react. The floor was stone and she saw some steps leading upwards. She strode across quickly, seeing the gun the man had in his jacket, but she ignored it. Craig had been right. She couldn't go in to Godfrey having killed half the people around him.

The steps were cold, but Kirsten moved almost soundlessly over them except for the occasional squelch from her sodden shoes. It was just when you stood in the wrong bit. Maybe there was a crack somewhere where the water had gathered or whatever else it was she had travelled through.

The steps turned round twice before they led out to a new floor. Kirsten walked along the red carpet, glancing down, and noticed that she was leaving marks. She kicked her shoes off and threw them under a chair. Her socks were sticky too, so she threw them off, preferring instead to walk along in bare feet.

Kirsten crept along. Moving off the red carpet, she again crossed stone floor, her feet feeling the chill of it. She heard a noise behind a door, and stepped back as someone walked in. Somebody was following him.

'Did they find out what the explosion was yet?'

'No, they're down there investigating . . .'

'Did you crap yourself?' the other man said. It was the last words the two men spoke before Kirsten hit one hard across the chin, knocking him out cold and then drove the other into the wall. As he hit it hard, she wrapped her arm around his neck, twisting him so that she could face the door and see if anyone else was coming in. The man slowly slipped away into unconsciousness as she held him tight, throttling him. *Don't kill anyone*, she thought. *It won't work if you kill them.*

Kirsten stole her way through the door and found herself in a large baronial room. At the far end, two large doors swung open, and Kirsten saw a man she recognised. He was old and dignified and she thought he walked with a limp. It was Godfrey. He was surrounded by four other men, all in suits, several of whom were now looking at the far end of the room wondering what a woman in sports gear was doing and why she smelt the way she did.

'Miss Stewart,' said Godfrey. 'What are you doing here?'

From behind Godfrey, Kirsten saw the bald head of a woman and Control stepped down in front of him.

'You two, guard him at all costs. Anderson, Jones, get her now. Shoot if you have to.'

Kirsten put her hands up in the air. 'Am no risk,' she said.

'I beg to differ,' said Control.

'I'm no risk, Godfrey.'

'Then explain yourself,' said Godfrey. 'Why are you here?'

'I'm on an errand from Anna Hunt.'

'Anna? Anna left the country. Isn't that right?' Godfrey turned to Control beside him, but he found himself flanked by the two men, keeping themselves between him, Godfrey, and Kirsten.

'There's been a lot of development since then. Anna and

Kirsten have been involved in the murder of many of our agents,' said Control.

'And you tell this to me now?'

'I have a data stick, Russian in origin,' said Kirsten, slowly stepping towards the pair.

'Keep your hands where they are,' Godfrey insisted, stepping past the bald woman.

'Look out,' shouted Kirsten for she saw Control suddenly reach inside her jacket. Before anyone could react, the two guards behind Godfrey had been shot dead and as the others spun around to the weapons fire, the bald woman put them both down.

'You've done me a great favour,' she said. 'I'll take that data stick.'

'And go where?' asked Godfrey. 'You'll never get out of here.'

'I don't intend to get out. I intend to assume command.'

'They'll never take orders from you above me,' said Godfrey. 'What do you mean by this?'

'If you're dead, and so is she, having been shot by me in an attempt to defend you, they'll take it from me and I'll take that stick and no one will be any of the wiser.'

The woman put her gun up towards Godfrey's face. Kirsten was too far away. If she started running, she'd never reach her in time. There was nothing nearby to throw. This was the end game and she was done. The woman had all the cards. When Kirsten looked at her, she understood Control was going to do it. Kirsten began to run.

'Goodbye Godfrey,' said the woman known as Control.

A single shot rang out and the Control tumbled to one side. Kirsten saw the blood pour from her head, running across the lush brown carpet. Godfrey stood like a statue as if half expecting his own demise. Almost instinctively, Kirsten ran over to the woman, taking the gun from her hand and throwing it away. She looked over to the double doors behind them where the shot had rung out from. There, dressed in jacket and trousers, was Craig, her London Man.

Chapter 25

Kirsten sat in the cell letting her feet dangle off the bunk bed. It had been several days of being dragged out for interviews, questioned over and over again about what had happened, why had it had happened, and the consistent question of where was Anna Hunt. Of course, Kirsten didn't tell them. She couldn't. The last she'd known, she had left Anna in Montrose, but she wouldn't be there now. As soon as she was mobile, Anna would make her own way, making sure she was clear in case anything went wrong. After all, she didn't know if Kirsten had made her plan a success. All she knew was that Kirsten was out there trying to sort out the problem.

Kirsten hadn't seen Dom or Carrie Anne either, and no one told her what had become of them. Dom, she felt reasonably happy about. He'd been taken in from the flyover at Stirling. It was very public, and the Russians couldn't have taken him from that point. They would have had to drag him away while there were so many police around. They'd have shot him right there and then instead. Dom knew the game was up. He'd made sure he got captured by their people. They were only pointing guns, not letting them off.

As far as Kirsten could tell, the message on the stick which had been recovered by Anna Hunt must have contained some sort of message identifying the sender; whether it showed this by where the information came from, who had access, or whether it was by having a code name on it, Kirsten did not know. But Russia deemed that when it had gone missing, it was essential to get it back. Of course, they would deny all knowledge, and whoever was working for them would be removed.

Kirsten, having seen the bald woman die in front of her, had woken up on several nights with that same moment, the moment when she couldn't reach Godfrey, the moment when she was probably going to die herself. And then he'd arrive like a knight in shining armour. Craig had said nothing either, and in fact, he had taken Kirsten's arms behind her and handed her over to the authorities. There was no get-out-quick. For a brief moment, Kirsten thought Godfrey would look at the information on the stick and she'd be out in the afternoon, sharing tea and medals and being thanked for a jolly good job done. Instead, she was inside a jail cell, and got only visits to a small room with some rather intimidating men who had broken up the solitude.

You got three square meals a day though, she thought, chuckling to herself. She often thought it was the least Godfrey could do to turn up and say, 'Thanks for warning me.' However, Kirsten had probably put his life in danger, barging in like that, but she had no idea that Control would be there.

Kirsten jumped up off her bunk, dropped to the floor, and started doing her press-up count. She went onto one arm to do thirty, then thirty on the other arm. She followed this with sit-ups. Then she jogged on the spot. Then she did sprints back and forward across the cell, only able to take a couple of steps at the time before turning and pushing back.

Over the next hour, she worked through some of her martial arts routines, centering herself before launching out kicks and turns, a combination of punches thrown out to the air. By the end of it, she was sweating, and her hair dripped out behind her, not in a ponytail, for everything had been taken off her that she could tie around any part of herself.

When she sat down next on the bunk, a tray of food was slid in through the flap in the bottom of the door. Kirsten went over, bent down, and took the water that was in the cup and then looked at the meat and potatoes. Frankly, it didn't look good, but she had it anyway, knowing she had to keep her strength. Inside the cells, she was unaware of what time of day it was, and her watch had been taken off her. Having been fatigued from her workout, she decided to sleep but was rudely awoken with the door crashing open, and two men marching in. Beyond the men was Godfrey.

'I hardly think these two are necessary,' said Kirsten. 'If I was out to kill you, I'd have dropped you when we were back at the castle.'

Godfrey laughed. 'Of course,' he said. 'But if you don't give them something to do, they stand around here like a waste of money. You two, out!'

'Shall I close the door, sir? I don't recommend it.'

'What? And leave her the opportunity to escape? Better one to die than to have our latest convict disappear.'

'Yes, sir,' said the man, and closed the door behind him.

Godfrey made his way over to Kirsten and sat down beside her on the bed.

'I apologise for the way things have turned out, but it's

routine. You came out of nowhere, so we had to check through everything. It's taken a while to decode what was on the stick, but the good news is, it's been very useful. I've also managed to rat out a few other people, one or two we didn't get to in time.'

'They've escaped,' said Kirsten.

'No, seems their masters didn't like the idea of them being identified either. Two were found deceased, another one missing a head, quite an ordeal, I think. Not sure it was very pleasant what happened to them before their demise either.'

Kirsten nodded and tried not to think about the method of dispatch of these traitors. 'I take it that the information on the stick was useful, lets you know more about Anna.'

'Anna Hunt has got a lot to thank you for.'

'Anna Hunt owes me nothing,' said Kirsten. 'She's my boss. I was watching her back.'

'You were sent to kill her, a cold order out of the blue. Would've been your first assassination. When she recruited you, Anna said, you were a woman who really thinks.'

'But you took me anyway,' said Kirsten, laughing.

'When Anna Hunt says you think, I would take you any day of the week. Anna infiltrated what was a disease at the core. The woman you knew as Control was running it all. She had several other agents with her, many sent out after you to check where you were, what you were doing, and, hopefully, lead to Anna Hunt. If she had simply asked questions, you might have not kept everything so closed, and opened up quicker, to ask why you were after Anna, exposing Control to others. But because she sent you on a kill mission, and she told you that you had to be dark about it, you stayed that way.'

Kirsten sat forward on the edge of the bed, stood up, and

walked across her cell before turning around and looking at Godfrey. 'But we got lucky though, didn't we? I mean, if Craig hadn't been there.'

'He trusted the right person,' said Godfrey, 'but he had a belief in you. After all, he was sent to follow you, sent by Control, but he's another thinker too, another one of Anna's recruits. I put a great deal in what Anna says, and that's because I've had the results over the years. This time, one of her recruits exposed a major network of spies within our group, and the other saved my life and yours. I believe you told him to stay away and not get involved.'

'I did.'

'Why?' asked Godfrey. 'Surely, you could have brought him in as an ally. He said you had him interrogated.'

'And he came up clean,' said Kirsten, 'and I was going in alone. I had already lost Dom and Carrie Anne. I didn't know where Justin was.'

'Then you needed to reach outside of your group and trust someone else. Thankfully, he was able to think beyond you.'

Kirsten hung her head dwelling on what had been said by Godfrey.

'Cheer up,' said Godfrey. 'It all worked out, didn't it? But I would say this, you're well aware relationships are not meant to happen within our teams.'

'Of course, instruction on probably day one or two of our training.'

'And an instruction that always gets ignored,' said Godfrey. 'Young men and women charging around in the heat of things. Yes, it's going to happen, but for most of them, they can keep it in their head. It's just sex. Can you do that?'

Kirsten bit her lip.

'No,' said Godfrey. 'Not with this one. Is it? You've done me a great favour, a great service, not just this time, but on previous occasions. The two of you work at different ends of the country. God knows why you want to make it work at that sort of distance, but we're not islands, and we don't live alone. But if you're going to make it work, be prepared. Someday it'll hurt and worse than this.'

'Worse?' said Kirsten. 'You weren't the one that had him interrogated. Dom, to his credit, did a thorough job but he wasn't keen on it. I could tell.'

'No,' said Godfrey, 'but you inspire loyalty. You're aware of that. Apparently, Dom went off on his own with no backup, running a sneak play. Well, he took all the heat, except he got more heat than he expected. Then Carrie Anne, sacrificing herself so you could get away. That's what my interrogator said over these last few days. Said you felt guilty about that one.'

'Have you heard from them?' said Kirsten.

'I have heard from an aquarium in North Queensferry who seem to believe that a couple of terrorists blew out their underwater tank, destroying a feature attraction.'

'Was a tough call, sir,' said Hope. 'We kind of got ourselves trapped. Justin got taken, we think. Either that or he had got spooked and had to run, although he doesn't spook easy.'

'No, he doesn't, and to be honest, he left a trail of two bodies on the way out. They came for him in numbers, so he had no option. He had no time to call.'

'So, he is alive?' said Kirsten.

'You don't get rid of Mr Chivers easily. He said he was struggling to locate you after that. Instead, he rooted back, picked up his old boss.'

'And Anna? Is Anna well?'

'Still recovering from her shoulder, or at least that's what I've heard. You can ask her how she is yourself. Upstairs in ten minutes. I'm going to see the circle.'

'The circle?' asked Kirsten.

'Yes,' said Godfrey, 'that's what we call ourselves. Rather dramatic, isn't it? It's just senior management. It appears that a few of them refused to take Anna's call. When she was out in the cold, a few of them seemed to believe Control.'

'Did you believe?'

'No, but I didn't get the chance to disbelieve either. The trouble with Control was that she kept it all from me. It's not unusual not to be briefed, but what she was running was large. I was investigating or trying to, what happened at Aberdeen, but everything moved so fast. That's why I called conference to come up to the castle, and then you showed up. Still,' said Godfrey, 'all's well that ends well. I'll see you upstairs. Anna will be along to pick you up in a moment.'

'Dom, Carrie Anne?'

Godfrey spun around, almost absent-mindedly. 'Oh, God, dear yes. Fine, fine. Our people got to them first.'

'But that wasn't your people with Carrie Anne, was it? They were shooting. They were coming to kill.'

'That's correct, but my people were outside at that point, or at least some of our good people. She left some problems down below before she stepped into our van to be taken away,' said Godfrey. 'Another two, I couldn't interrogate. Very effective woman. Quite remarkable.'

Kirsten thought for a moment that the man was dwelling almost too long. 'Speaking of relationships,' he said, 'ask Anna about when she was twenty-one and the dashing man who was racing up the section. Like I said, lovely woman, remarkable. You want to leave it alone now.' With that, Godfrey turned, knocked on the door of the cell and watched it open.

'As I said, Anna will be here for you. All right, boys, with me, you can leave the door open. Miss Stewart is no longer our prisoner. She is once again our colleague.'

Kirsten watched him leave, breathing a deep sigh of relief. She knew he would never tell her everything about what was on that stick. She'd never know all the ins and outs, but she knew what she needed to know. Dom, Carrie Anne, Justin, and Anna—they were all safe.

Kirsten sat on the edge of the bed, swinging her legs underneath it. Anna was five minutes late. Godfrey had said ten minutes and it was now fifteen. Then Kirsten heard the crisp walk of what was rather thick heels on the back of a smart set of black shoes. The head hung forward, her feet swinging underneath her. Kirsten first clocked the shoes and then followed the legs up to the suit and the dark hair at the top.

'Are you okay?' asked Anna.

'We got there. Godfrey seems rather pleased.'

'Pleased?' said Anna. 'He's pissed off. Not at you, not at me. He's had several double agents running within this organisation. We're going upstairs where there's going to be conversations. One or two things you're going to be privy to that won't leave the room.'

'A thank you?'

'No,' said Anna, 'it's not. Godfrey doesn't work like that. He doesn't hand out sweeties just because you've been rather a good girl. You're up there to get eyes on faces. This is Godfrey letting them know you and me are in the room of the inner circle. He's warning them: you step out of line, he's sending the hounds after you.'

'Hounds? Bloodhounds?' Kirsten laughed. 'Is that what they see us as?'

'You're as dogged as they come,' said Anna, 'that's why I like you.'

Kirsten looked at the woman and saw no glimmer of a laugh. 'What about your shoulder?' she asked. 'What about the wound?'

'It's there,' said Anna, 'and frankly, it hurts like hell, but I'm not going up there in a sling. They're going to see me as me, ready to kick their arse if it happens, the cold-blooded woman at Godfrey's side.'

'What do you want from me? What pose would you like me to take?'

'No pose,' said Anna, 'you just look at them. You look at them with those eyes that you've got, the ones that are searching. He's taking you up there to let them know that you're one of the special ones, the ones who can work things out. The ones that will follow through.'

'And then what?' asked Kirsten.

'And then you're going to Heathrow. You're going to get on one of the company planes and you go back up to Inverness.'

'Heathrow?' Said Kirsten.

'Yes, you're in London.'

'I have no idea where I am. They knocked me out when they transported me.'

'Of course, they did, but I'll take a ride up the road with you, although I'm keeping the jet, coming back to Edinburgh.'

'So, I'll just go up like this?' Said Kirsten. She looked down at the fatigues she was wearing, little more than bedclothes.

'They'll bring your clothes in in a minute. I did tell them to get that leather jacket of yours cleaned. I think they found it in a car somewhere.'

Kirsten smiled. 'There was a bit of a trail going backwards, I hope that . . . '

'We have friends, and those poor people had thieves come in there to take their stuff. But you get changed and then we'll walk up.'

'Okay,' said Kirsten, and she sat back down on the bed.

'Oh, one more thing,' said Anna before she left the room, 'thanks.'

'For what? Not putting a bullet in you?'

'No, thanks for Linda. I know I said it before, but everything else I could live with, not that.'

Twenty minutes later, Kirsten walked along beside the impressive figure of Anna Hunt. Double doors were opened, and they marched into a room with a large round table. At the far end was Godfrey who gave Anna a deliberate grin. For the next five minutes, Godfrey spoke about what had happened. Over and over, he chastised those around him for not being able to see it occurring. Most of what was going on went over Kirsten's head, as she focused on the faces around the table. Men and women of a slightly older age, but she could see the fear in their eyes. When Kirsten turned around to walk out of the double doors, she noted that Anna didn't turn quickly. Instead, Anna stopped, stared at each one of the inner circle in their seats, glaring at them, before she finally turned to Godfrey, gave a wry smile, and a nod of the head. Blimey, Kirsten thought, never would she cross that woman.

Epilogue

I t was late. There was a light shining into the room through the loosely closed curtains that shone into Kirsten's eyes. Blinking, she moved her head clear of it, then looked up to see the clock. Five a.m. The last time she'd seen it, she was sure it said three. It had said one before that. Possibly eleven. She'd gone to bed, she reckoned, at about seven, the words 'nothing on the telly' still ringing in her ears.

Earlier, she received a message. *Take yourself off to this lodge, high up in the Cairngorms.* All around her, she could see snow when she had arrived, but there was no one else there. Once inside, she'd started a fire and when she'd opened the fridge, she'd seen the champagne. There was plenty of food, some steaks, and then she'd heard the doorbell ring.

Kirsten took her gun out, approached the door carefully, and opened it slowly. When the door had opened enough that she could see the face of the caller, she had struggled to maintain her composure. At first, she felt the tears begin to fall, and then she'd opened the door and saw the surprise on his face, and in her right hand was a gun.

She'd fallen forward, collapsing onto him, wrapping herself around him. He was dressed in one of his suits. Through bleary eyes, she'd seen first a smile, then a look of concern, and then a feeling she'd only known as home. After she'd stood there for a full minute clinging on to him, he'd reached down, swept her legs from under her, and carried her into the lodge. He'd placed her down on the sofa before closing the door and told her that she had an hour to get herself ready. She asked where she was going. He said nowhere. While she had been given instructions to go into the bedroom and to check the wardrobes, Craig had begun to cook in the kitchen.

Kirsten had never been one for dressing up. When she saw the backless number hanging in the wardrobe, she decided to embrace a bit of class for the evening. They had dined, looking out the window, watching the snowfall, and indulged in two of the bottles of wine. Several times she'd gone to speak, to tell him that she was sorry for what she did to him, for not trusting him. Each time, he put his finger up to her mouth and told her to be quiet.

There hadn't been much sleep that night, and they simply enjoyed their time together. Now at five, still feeling fatigued from the exertions of the evening, Kirsten fought between the idea of rolling back over or getting up. She felt like she wanted a bath, a shower of some sort, something or the other. When she looked back, he was asleep, snoring lightly.

Without embarrassment, she threw off the covers of the bed, strolled over to the bathroom, and turned on the shower. She climbed inside and began to let the water soak over her features. Slowly, she kept turning around. Every now and again, she would see the face of Control and the look of shock on Godfrey's face. Kirsten stood with her eyes shut, the water hitting the top of her shoulders, some going down her back, the rest down her front.

Then the shower curtain was whipped back. She opened her eyes to see the smiling face of Craig. He stepped into the shower with her, pulled the curtain back across, and embraced her. It was an hour later when they had dried, put on the dressing gowns that came with the lodge, and sat at the large window looking out to the snow-covered land. The sun was just coming up and Kirsten had made a large pot of black coffee.

'Godfrey says this happens a lot.'

'Really?' said Craig, 'We have some sort of a budget for it or something?'

'No,' said Kirsten, 'I guess it's hard to trust. He said most of the rest of them, it's just sex.'

'Well,' said Craig, 'I think that's definitely involved with us, isn't it?'

Kirsten laughed, 'But it is a lot more than that, isn't it?' She smiled as Craig nodded. Putting her coffee down, she stood up and looked out of the window, and then found Craig behind her, sending his arms under hers, wrapping her up tight, gently kissing her neck. As Kirsten enjoyed the moment, her eyes fanned across the snow outside, and she saw something.

There was something black, distinct, like a round cylindrical top and then something behind it, hooded.

'What the hell?' shouted Kirsten.

She turned, running across the room, leaving Craig in her wake. She burst the door open and ran across, unashamed in the snow, just a dressing gown on. She felt the cold coursing through her feet, but her eyes were fixed ahead. A figure began to run.

He had a parka on, a camera around his shoulders, a little backpack too. Whoever it was had a large start on her and was making for the road that had led up to the lodge. Kirsten ran hard but could see the person was going to reach the road before her. She heard the sound of a car engine fighting hard up the slope. As she got closer, she saw the Land Rover arrive, turn around, and then threw open a door for the person.

Kirsten sucked in huge drafts of cold air, driving her body on. She was tired from the night before, but still, she hunted the figure down. As he reached the Land Rover, she found herself diving and caught the foot of the man. He tripped. As she looked up from the snow, she saw an arm reach down, and pull him up into the Land Rover, which then drove off quickly.

Kirsten lay in the snow looking up. Just who had that been? Why photographs of her? What good was a photograph of her and Craig? When she felt the cold seep in from the snow across her chest, she lifted herself from nature's white blanket, wrapping the dressing around her as best she could, and quickly started making her way back. Craig met her three-quarters of the way there. He placed a coat around her, and together, they walked back into the lodge.

'Did you see who it was?' asked Craig.

Kirsten shook her head. Then she stood at the door, not allowing him to close it, looking out, and ignoring the light wind that was now blowing the cold air onto the wet front of her dressing gown.

'What was that about?' asked Craig.

She turned and looked at him, smiled briefly, and then kissed him, before she turned and look back out of the door, her face becoming worried. 'We upset someone, you and me. We upset someone. I have a feeling this may come back at me.'

Craig put his hand into hers, holding it tight. 'It's coming back at us,' he said. 'Us.'

Read on to discover the Patrick
Smythe series!

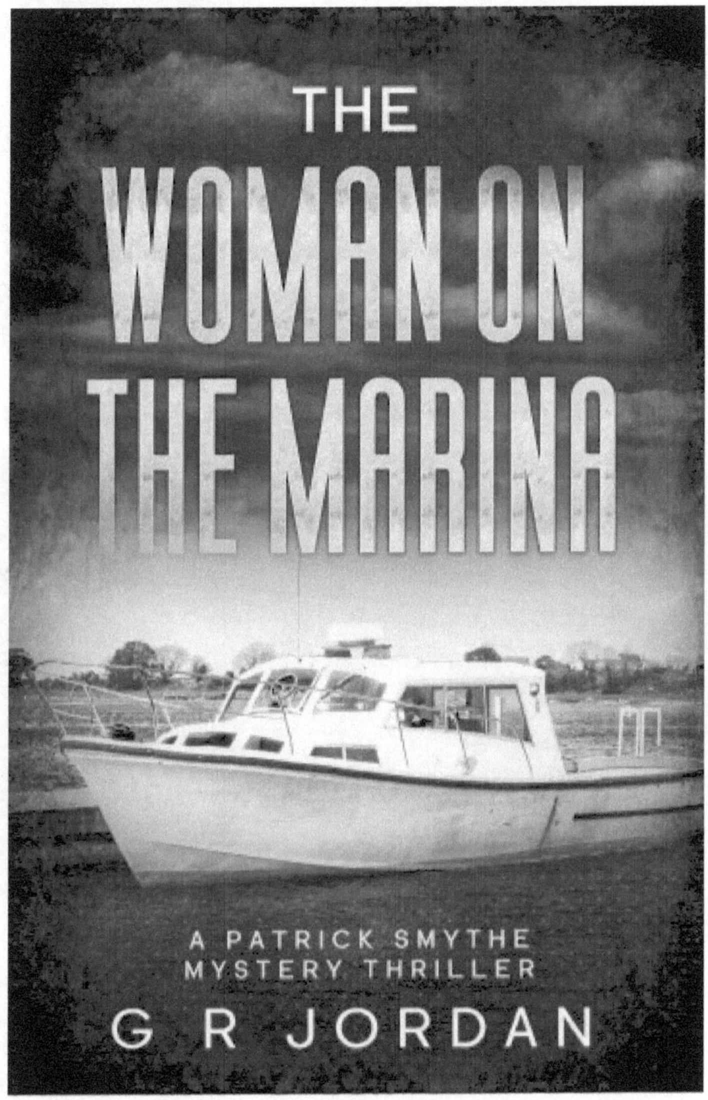

Start your Patrick Smythe journey here!

Patrick Smythe is a former Northern Irish policeman who

after suffering an amputation after a bomb blast, takes to the sea between the west coast of Scotland and his homeland to ply his trade as a private investigator. Join Paddy as he tries to work to his own ethics while knowing how to bend the rules he once enforced. Working from his beloved motorboat 'Craigantlet', Paddy decides to rescue a drug mule in this short story from the pen of G R Jordan.

Join G R Jordan's monthly newsletter about forthcoming releases and special writings for his tribe of avid readers and then receive your free Patrick Smythe short story.

Go to https://bit.ly/PatrickSmythe for your Patrick Smythe journey to start!

About the Author

GR Jordan is a self-published author who finally decided at forty that in order to have an enjoyable lifestyle, his creative beast within would have to be unleashed. His books mirror that conflict in life where acts of decency contend with self-promotion, goodness stares in horror at evil, and kindness blindsides us when we at our worst. Corrupting our world with his parade of wondrous and horrific characters, he highlights everyday tensions with fresh eyes whilst taking his methodical, intelligent mainstays on a roller-coaster ride of dilemmas, all the while suffering the banter of their provocative sidekicks.

A graduate of Loughborough University where he masqueraded as a chemical engineer but ultimately played American football, Gary had worked at changing the shape of cereal flakes and pulled a pallet truck for a living. Watching vegetables freeze at -40'C was another career highlight and he was also one of the Scottish Highlands "blind" air traffic controllers.

These days he has graduated to answering a telephone to people in trouble before telephoning other people to sort it out.

Having flirted with most places in the UK, he is now based in the Isle of Lewis in Scotland where his free time is spent between raising a young family with his wife, writing, figuring out how to work a loom and caring for a small flock of chickens. Luckily, his writing is influenced by his varied work and life experience as the chickens have not been the poetical inspiration he had hoped for!

You can connect with me on:
🌐 https://grjordan.com
https://facebook.com/carpetlessleprechaun

Subscribe to my newsletter:
✉ https://bit.ly/PatrickSmythe

Also by G R Jordan

G R Jordan writes across multiple genres including crime, dark and action adventure fantasy, feel good fantasy, mystery thriller and horror fantasy. Below is a selection of his work. Whilst all books are available across online stores, signed copies are available at his personal shop.

The Execution of Celebrity (A Kirsten Stewart Thriller #6)
https://grjordan.com/product/the-execution-of-celebrity
Television personalities suddenly disappear. A confluence of agents in the North of Scotland. Can Kirsten Stewart make the connection and prevent an on-air execution.

When Scottish celebrities begin to disappear, the police enlist the help of the Service to find the guilty parties. But Kirsten and her team are stretched as a flood of foreign agents seem to be massing in the Scottish Highlands. Can the team make the connection and stop a broadcast that will leave every citizen numb to their core?

Sometimes there is such a thing as bad publicity!

Cleared to Die (Highlands & Islands Detective Book 18)
https://grjordan.com/product/cleared-to-die
A dead controller killed alone in his tower. A climate of fear and coercion among employees and managers. Can Macleod enter the world of air traffic and bring a safe, orderly, and expeditious solution to the case?

When a commercial turboprop is forced to go-around on losing communication with Mull tower, the operations team find their oldest controller dead at his post. Amidst a furore over a change of working, Macleod and McGrath find a company in turmoil and with grudges to settle. As the sides are unmasked and the stakes known, can the pair see through the anger and disgruntlement, to bring a brutal killer to justice?

Silence is golden... unless you need to land!

The Disappearance of Russell Hadleigh (Patrick Smythe Book 1)

https://grjordan.com/product/the-disappearance-of-russell-hadleigh

A retired judge fails to meet his golf partner. His wife calls for help while running a fantasy play ring. When Russians start co-opting into a fairly-traded clothing brand, can Paddy untangle the strands before the bodies start littering the golf course?

In his first full novel, Patrick Smythe, the single-armed former policeman, must infiltrate the golfing social scene to discover the fate of his client's husband. Assisted by a young starlet of the greens, Paddy tries to understand just who bears a grudge and who likes to play in the rough, culminating in a high stakes showdown where lives are hanging by the reaction of a moment. If you love pacey action, suspicious motives and devious characters, then Paddy Smythe operates amongst your kind of people.

Love is a matter of taste but money always demands more of its suitor.

Surface Tensions (Island Adventures Book 1)
https://grjordan.com/product/surface-tensions
Mermaids sighted near a Scottish island. A town exploding in anger and distrust. And Donald's got to get the sexiest fish in town, back in the water.

"Surface Tensions" is the first story in a series of Island adventures from the pen of G R Jordan. If you love comic moments, cosy adventures and light fantasy action, then you'll love these tales with a twist. Get the book that amazon readers said, "perfectly captures life in the Scottish Hebrides" and that explores "human nature at its best and worst".

Something's stirring the water!

Corpse Reviver (A Contessa Munroe Mystery #1)

https://grjordan.com/product/corspe-reviver

A widowed Contessa flees to the northern waters in search of adventure. An entrepreneur dies on an ice pack excursion. But when the victim starts moonlighting from his locked cabin, can the Contessa uncover the true mystery of his death?

Catriona Cullodena Munroe, widow of the late Count de Los Palermo, has fled the family home, avoiding the scramble for title and land. As she searches for the life she always wanted, the Contessa, in the company of the autistic and rejected Tiff, must solve the mystery of a man who just won't let his business go.

Corpse Reviver is the first murder mystery involving the formidable and sometimes downright rude lady of leisure and her straight talking niece. Bonded by blood, and thrown together by fate, join this pair of thrill seekers as they realise that flirting with danger brings a price to pay.